**Hi, Parents!**

Your child's love of reading starts here, with HarperAlley's **I Can Read *Comics*!**

**I Can Read *Comics*** introduces children to the world of graphic novel storytelling and encourages visual literacy in emerging readers. Comics inspire reader engagement unlike any other format. They ask readers to infer and answer questions, like:

1. What do I read first? Image or text?
2. Why is this word balloon shaped this way, and that word balloon shaped that way?
3. Why is a character making that facial expression? Are they happy, angry, excited, sad?

From the comics your child reads with you to the first comic they read on their own, there are **I Can Read *Comics*** for every stage of reading:

**LEVEL 1**

Simple stories for shared reading.

**LEVEL 2**

Engaging stories for children reading on their own.

**LEVEL 3**

Complex stories for independent readers.

The magic of graphic novel storytelling lies between the gutters. Unlock the magic with…

# I Can Read *Comics*!

Visit **ICanRead.com** for information on enriching your child's reading experience.

# I Can Read *Comics* Cartooning Basics

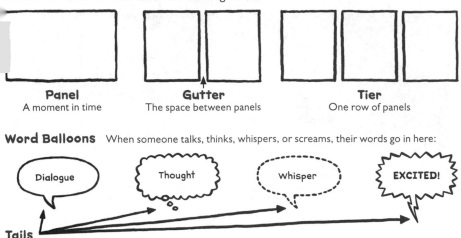

**Panel**
A moment in time

**Gutter**
The space between panels

**Tier**
One row of panels

**Word Balloons** When someone talks, thinks, whispers, or screams, their words go in here:

Dialogue    Thought    Whisper    EXCITED!

**Tails**
Point to whoever is talking / thinking / whispering / screaming / etc.

## A quick how-to-read comics guide:

In a **panel**, read the text on the **left** first.

Then, read the text on the right.

## Remember to...

Read the text along with the image, paying close attention to the character's acting, the action, and/or the scene. Every little detail matters!

### No dialogue? No problem!

If there is no dialogue within a panel, take the time to read the image. Visual cues are just as important as text, so don't forget about them!

On a page, **start here**, in the **top left** corner!

After that, read the panel immediately to the **right**.

When you're done up there, come down here and read **this** panel **next**!

ME NEXT! ME NEXT!

You're almost there...

YOU MADE IT! You just read a comic page!

YAY!

*For Yiayia and Pappou,*
*for giving me the time to make this book*
*—V.F.*

HarperAlley is an imprint of HarperCollins Publishers.
I Can Read® and I Can Read Book® are trademarks of HarperCollins Publishers.

Friendbots: Blink and Block Bug Each Other
Copyright © 2021 by Vicky Fang
All rights reserved. Printed in the United States of America.

Library of Congress Control Number: 2021939618
ISBN 978-0-06-304948-2 (trade bdg.) — ISBN 978-0-06-304947-5 (pbk.)

Book design by Joe Merkel
21 22 23 24 25  LSCC  10 9 8 7 6 5 4 3 2 1  ❖  First Edition

# FRIENDBOTS

## Blink and Block
## Bug Each Other

by Vicky Fang

HARPER
alley

An Imprint of HarperCollinsPublishers

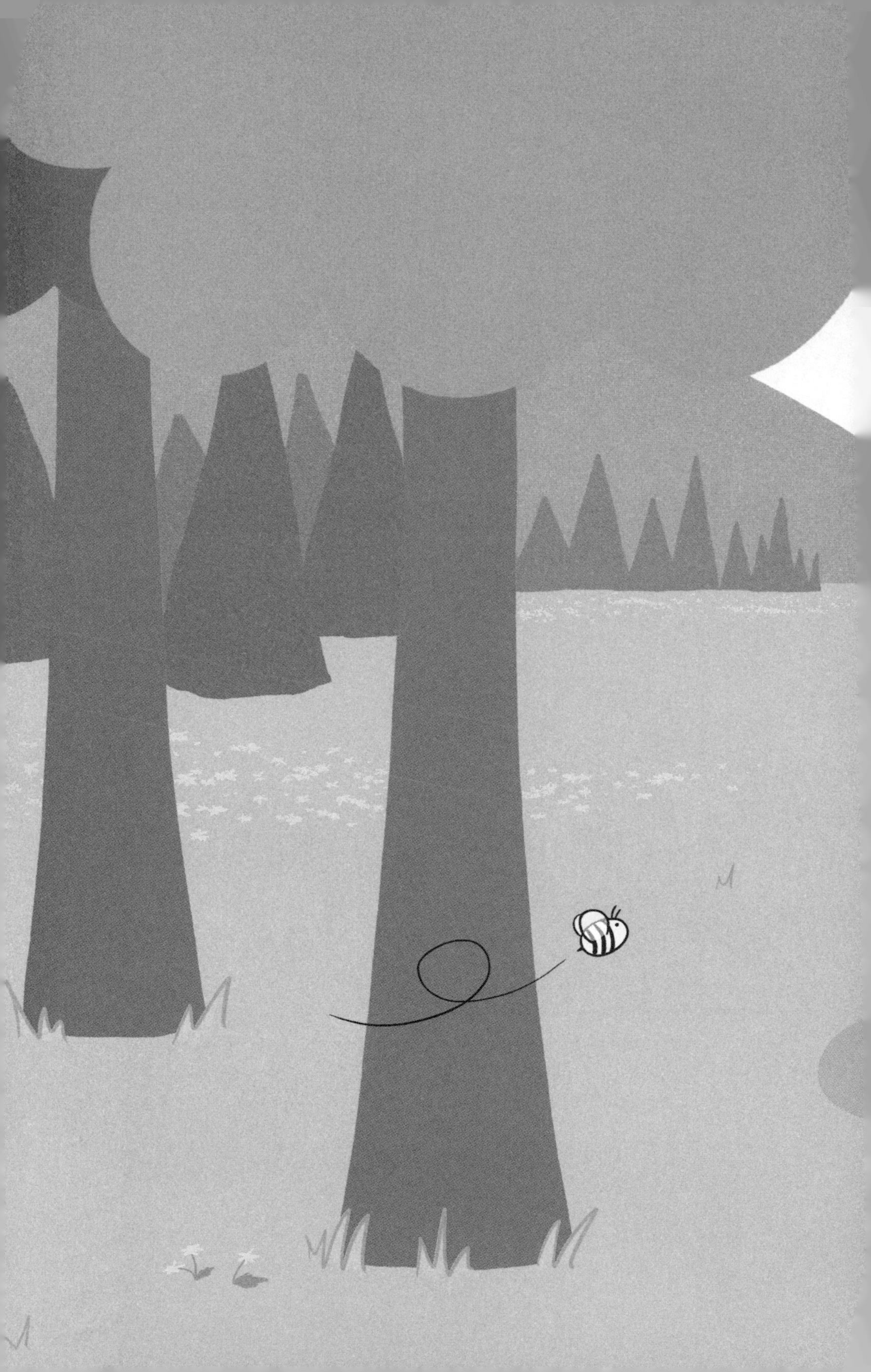

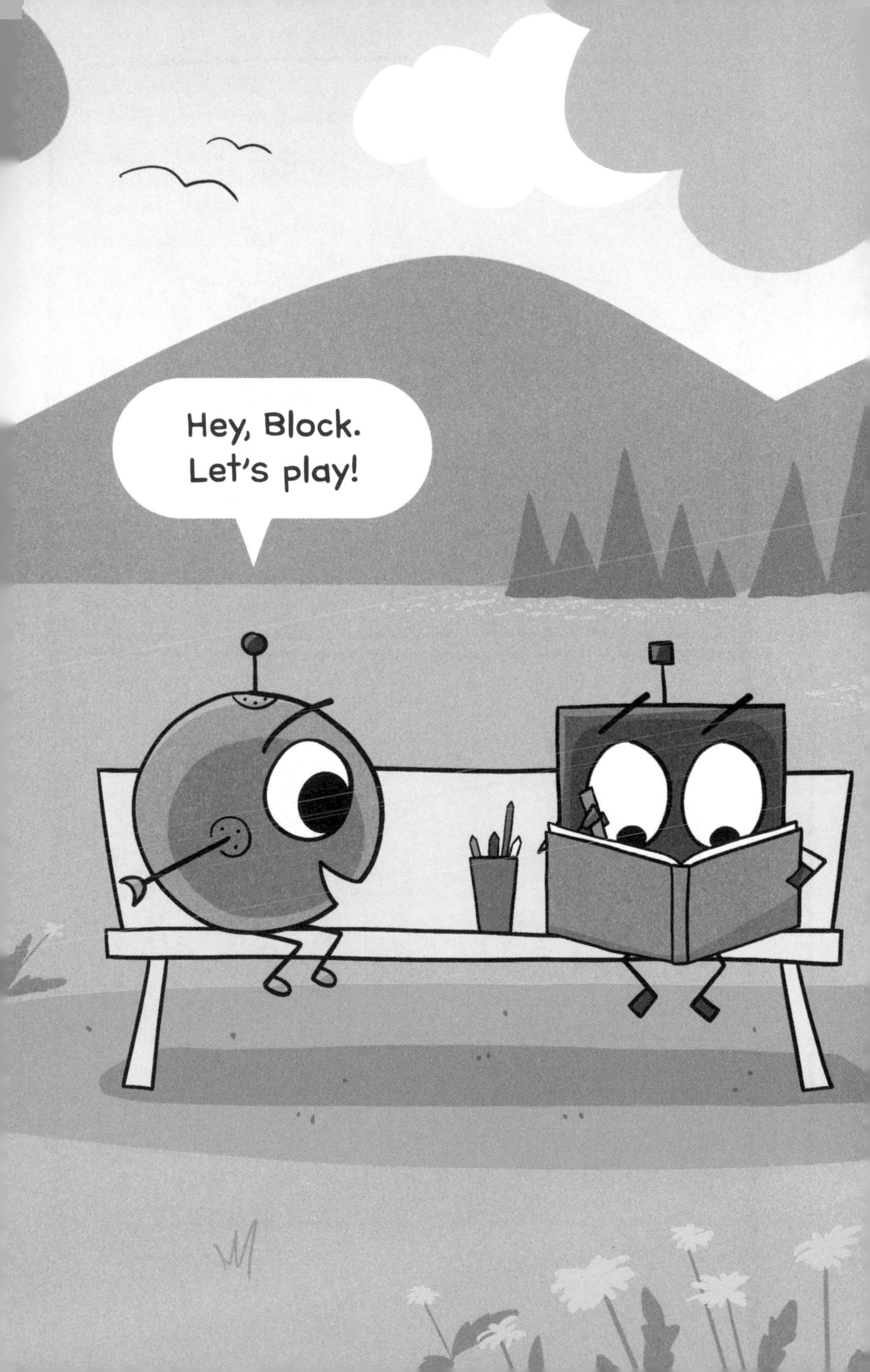
Hey, Block.
Let's play!

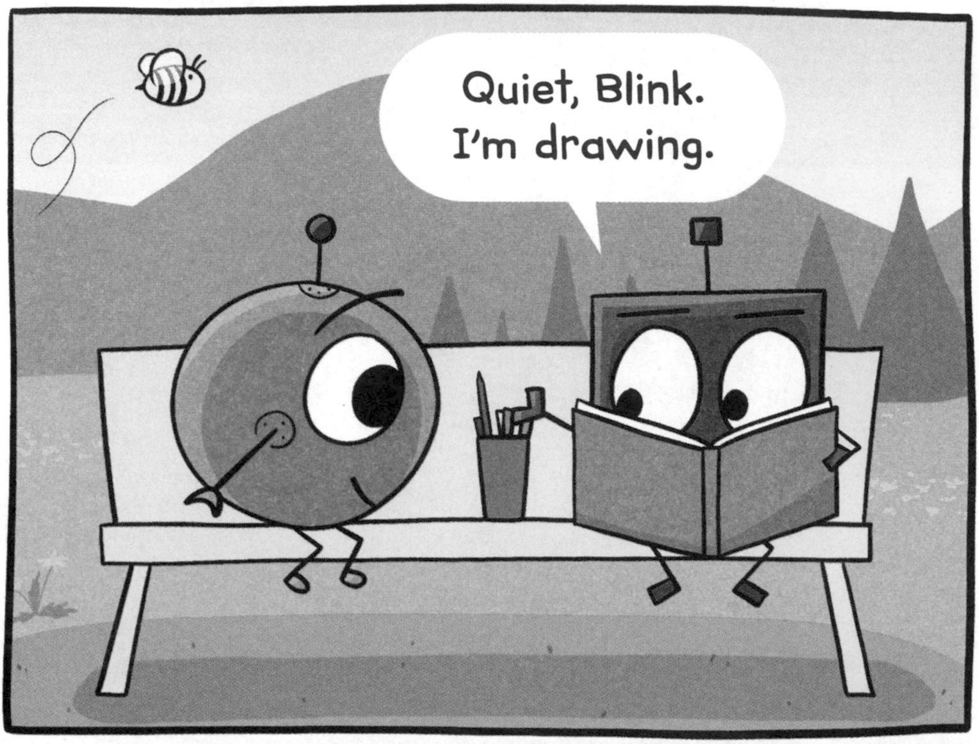
Quiet, Blink.
I'm drawing.

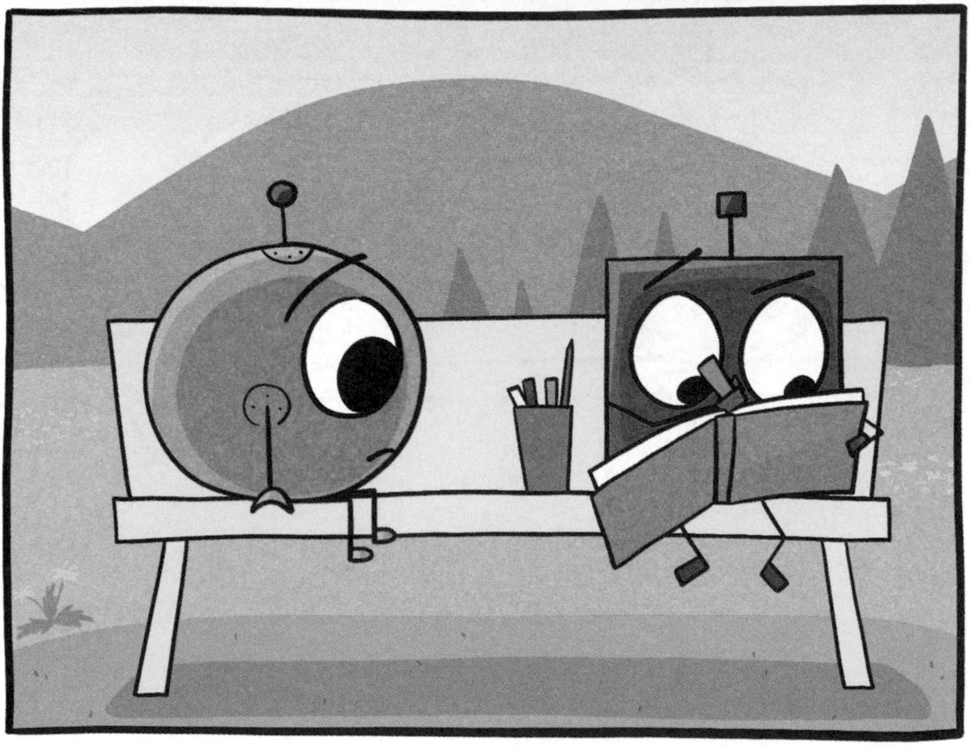

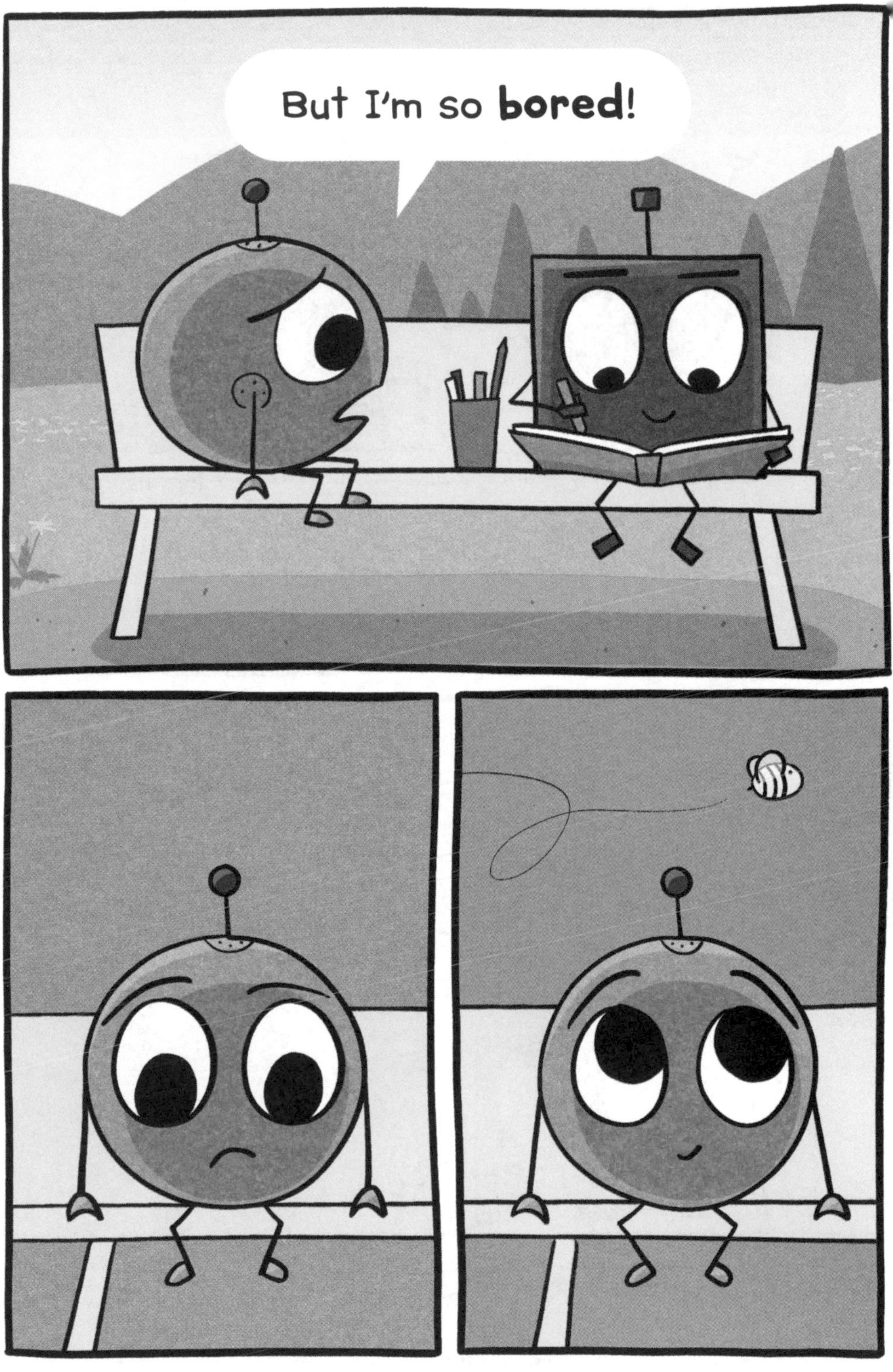
But I'm so **bored**!

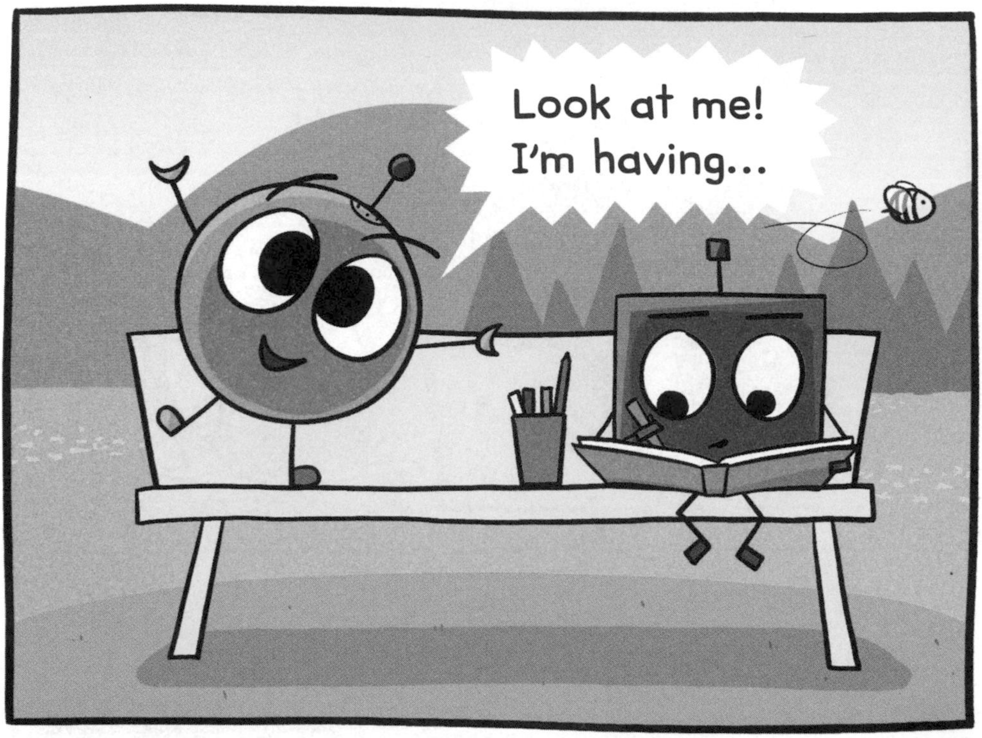
Look at me!
I'm having...

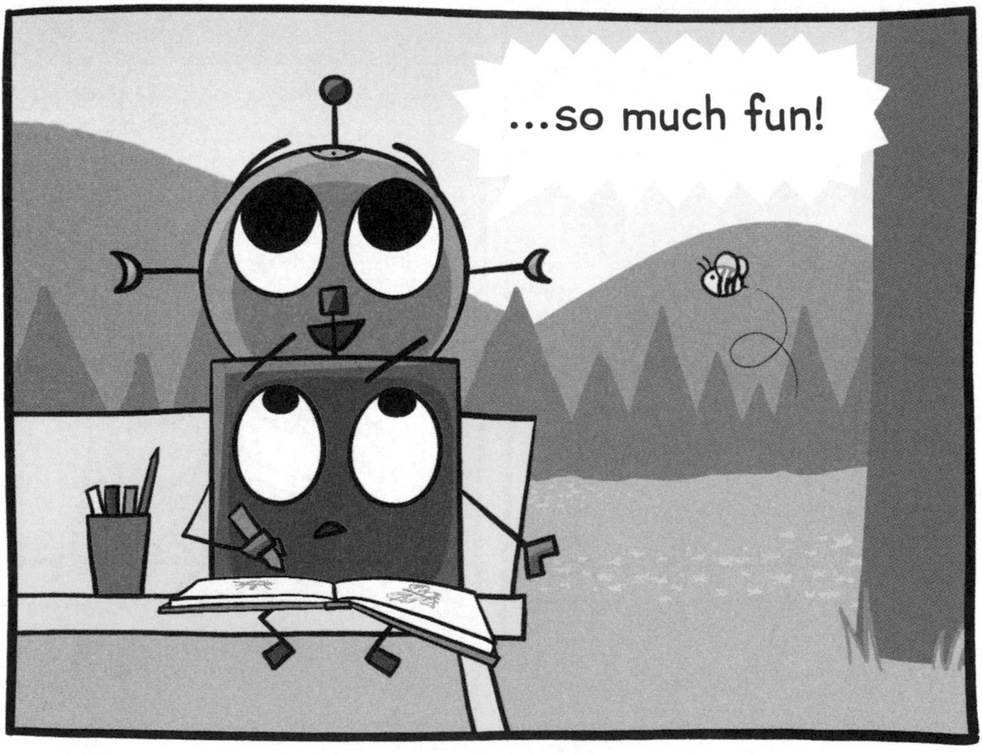
...so much fun!

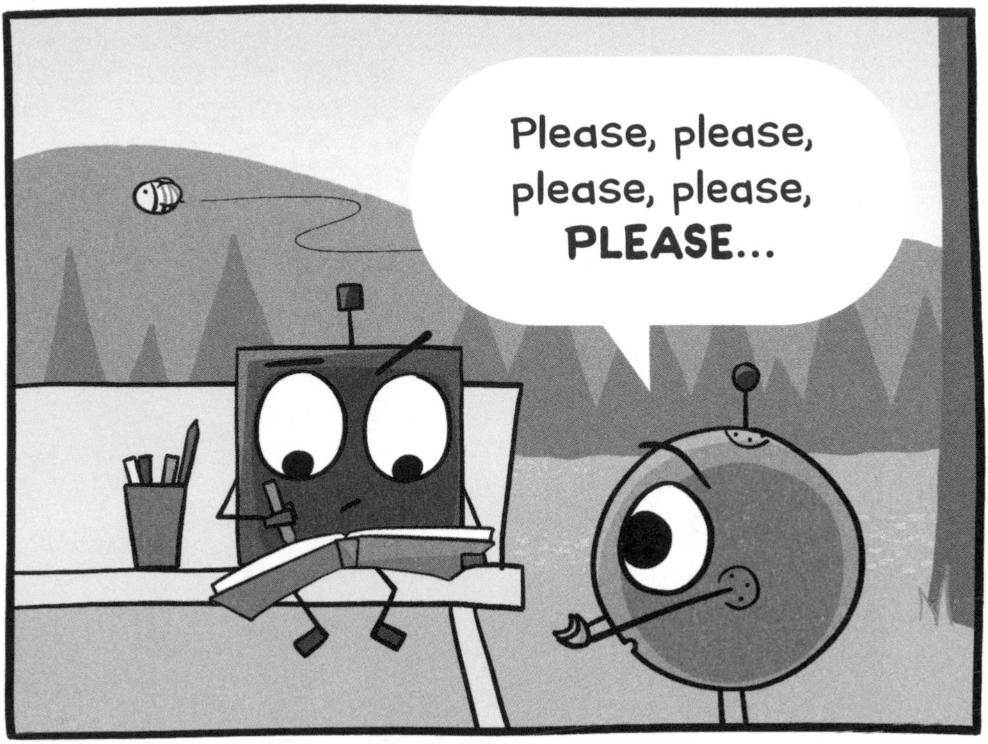
Please, please, please, please, **PLEASE**...

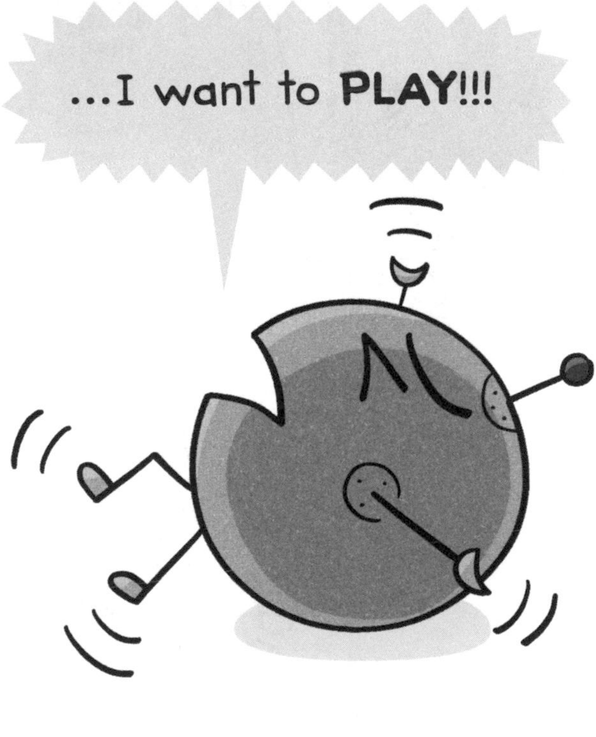
...I want to **PLAY**!!!

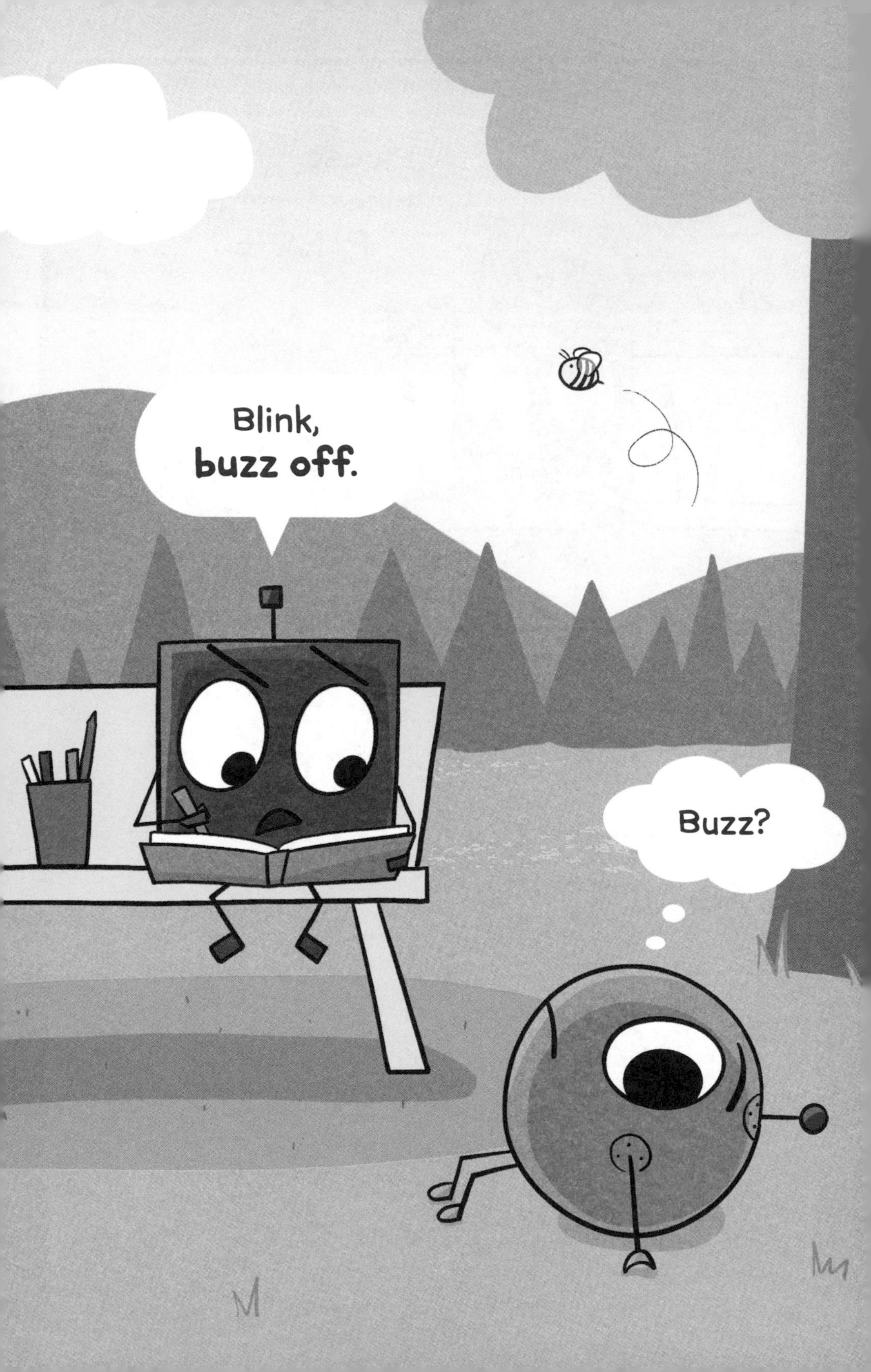
Blink,
**buzz off.**
Buzz?

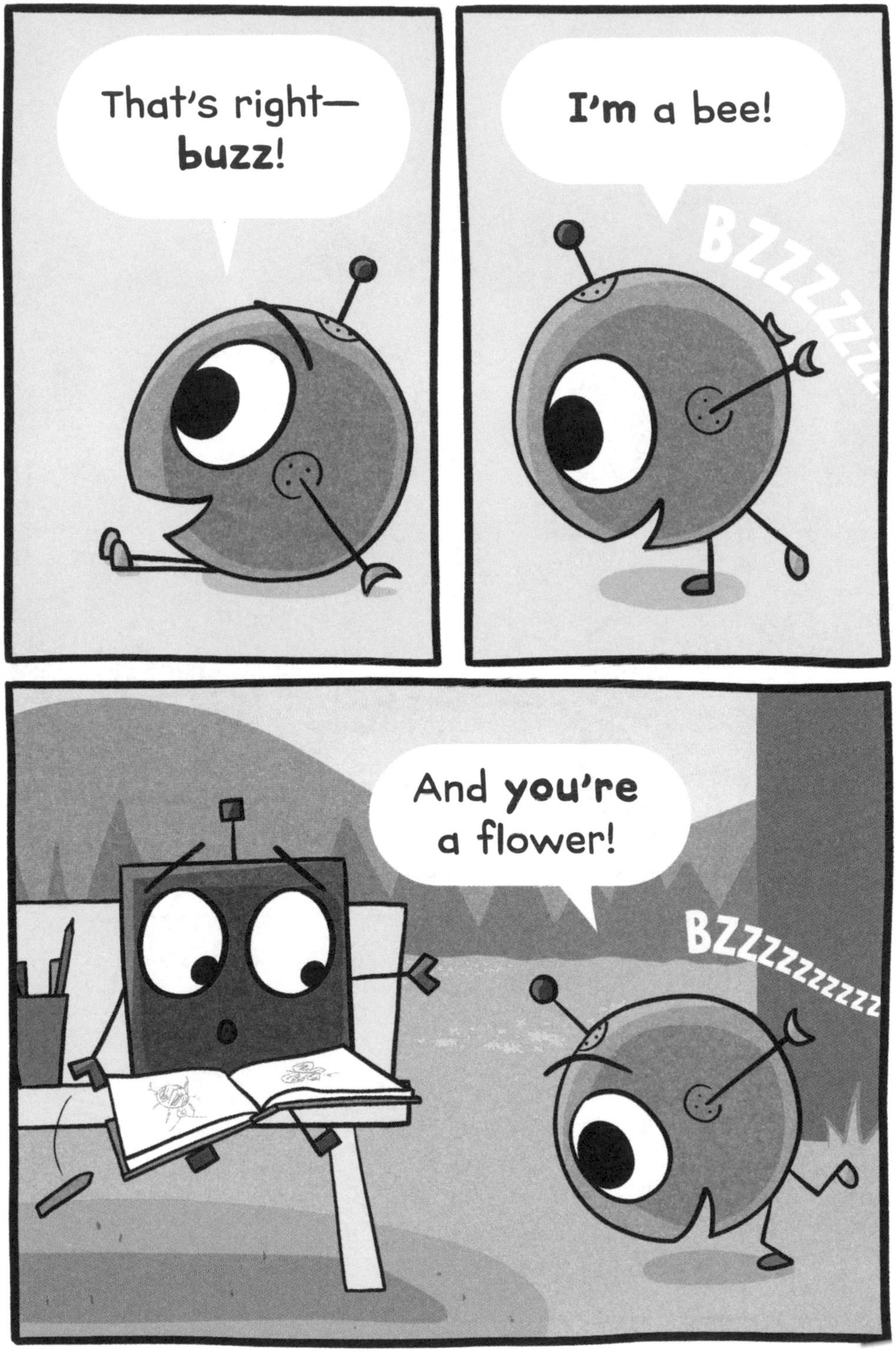
That's right—
**buzz!**
**I'm** a bee!
BZZZZZZZ
And **you're**
a flower!
BZZZZZZZZZZ

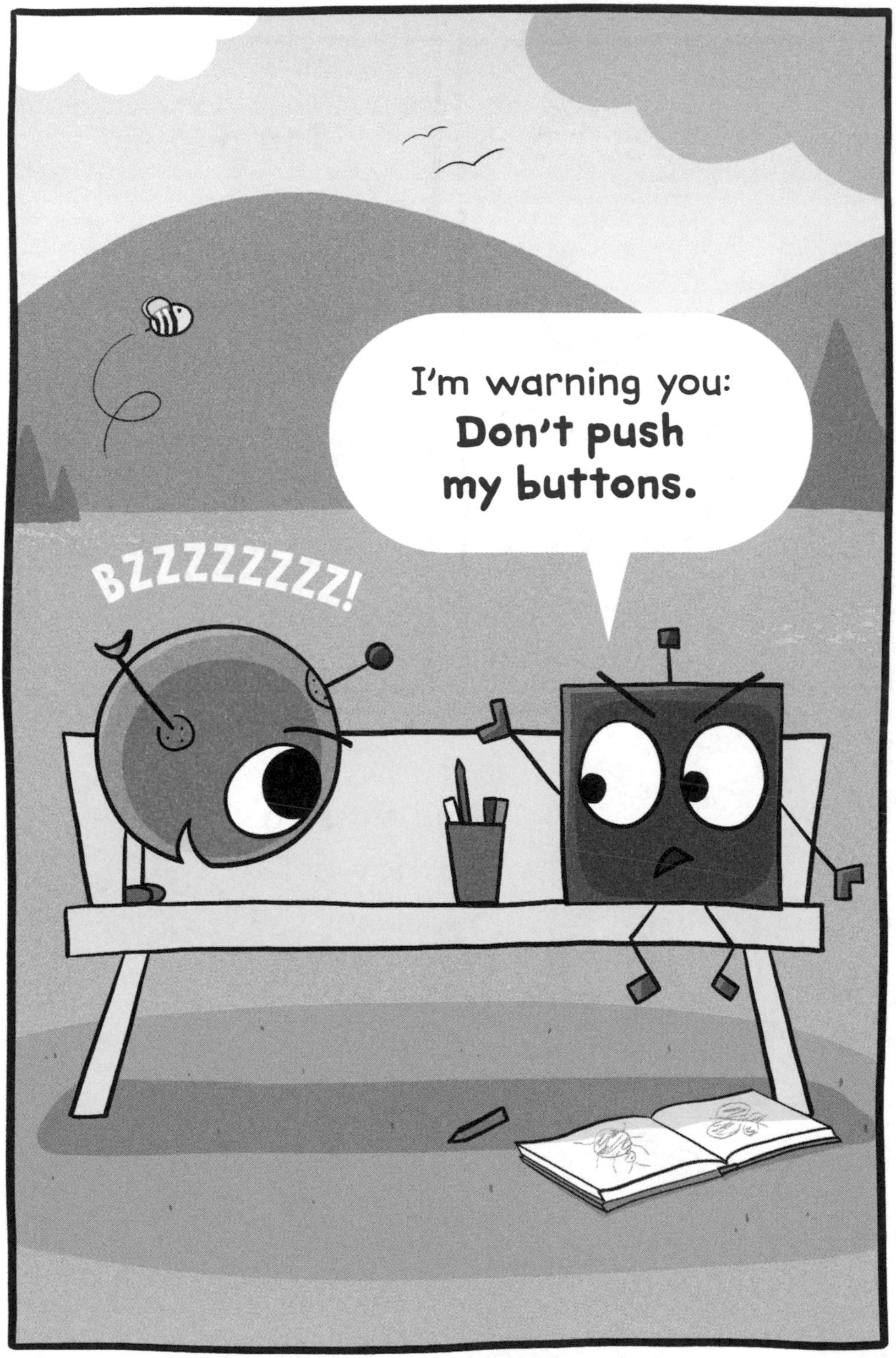
BZZZZZZZZ!
I'm warning you:
**Don't push my buttons.**

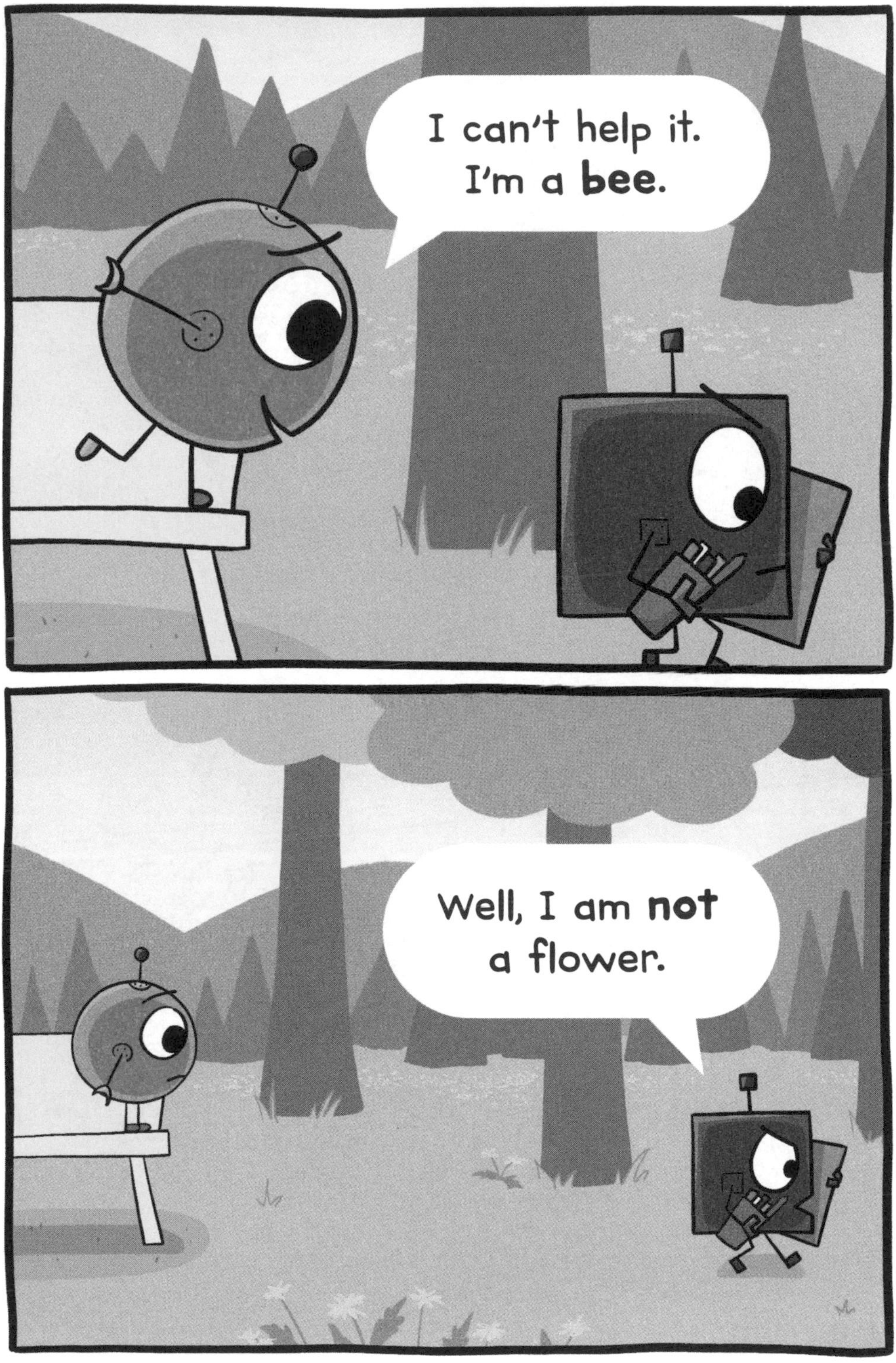
I can't help it. I'm a **bee**.
Well, I am **not** a flower.

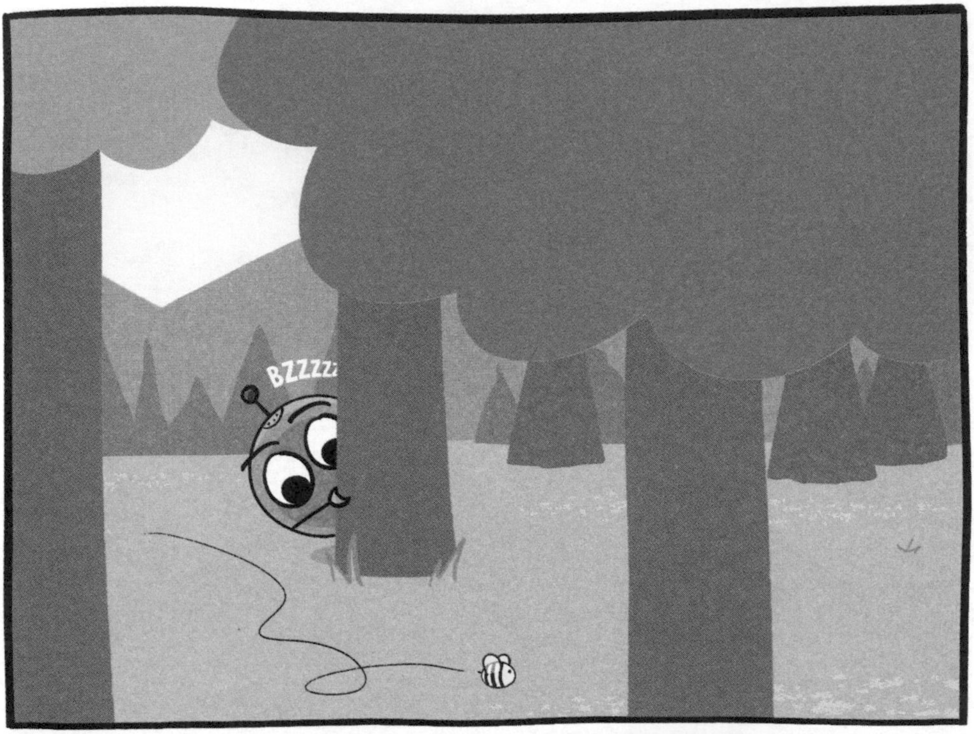
BZZZZ

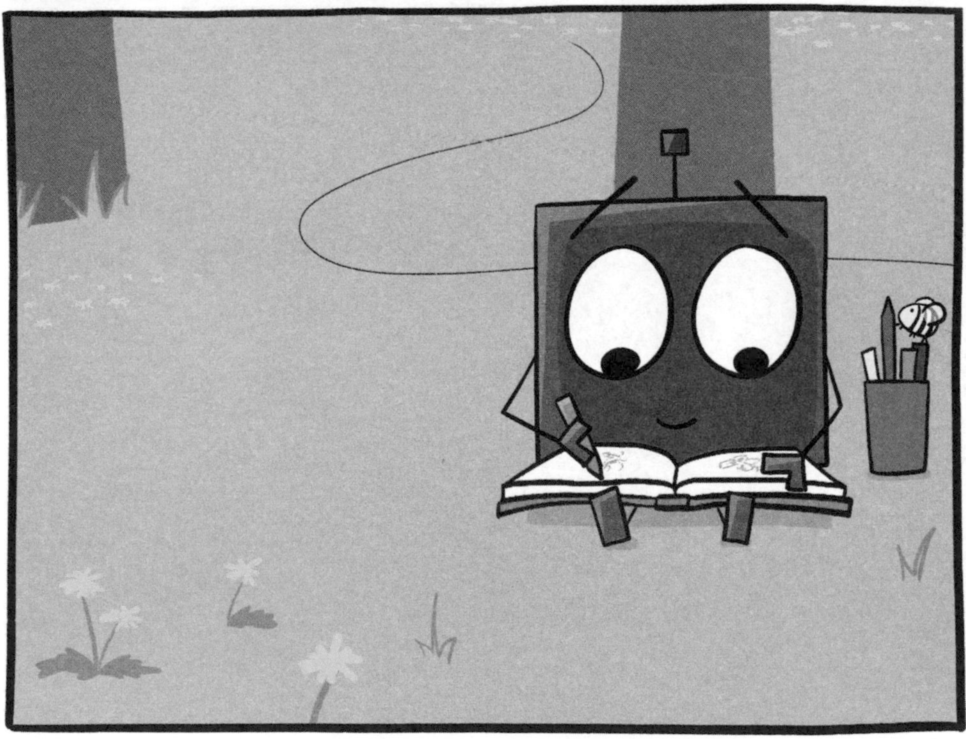

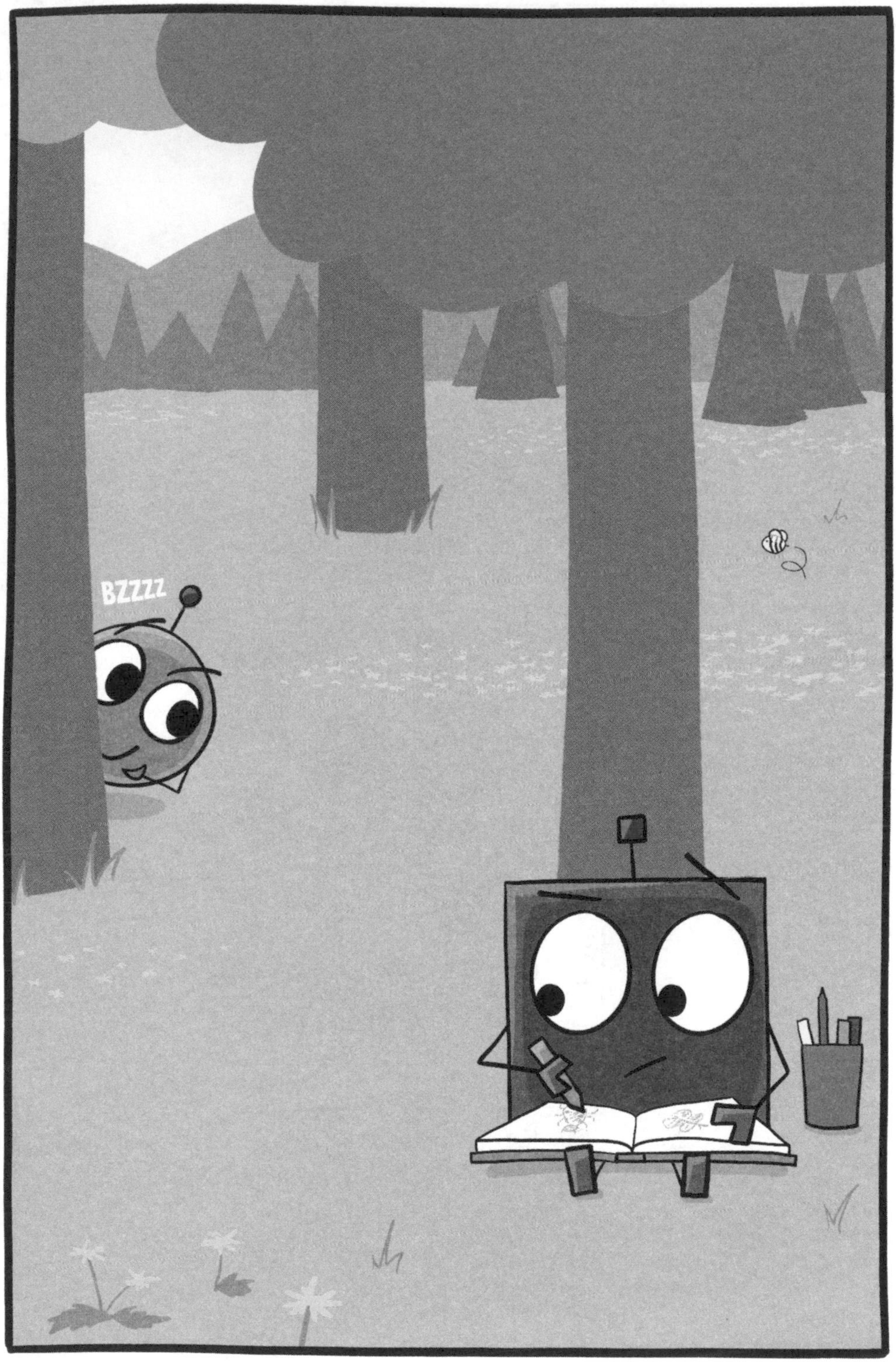
BZZZZ

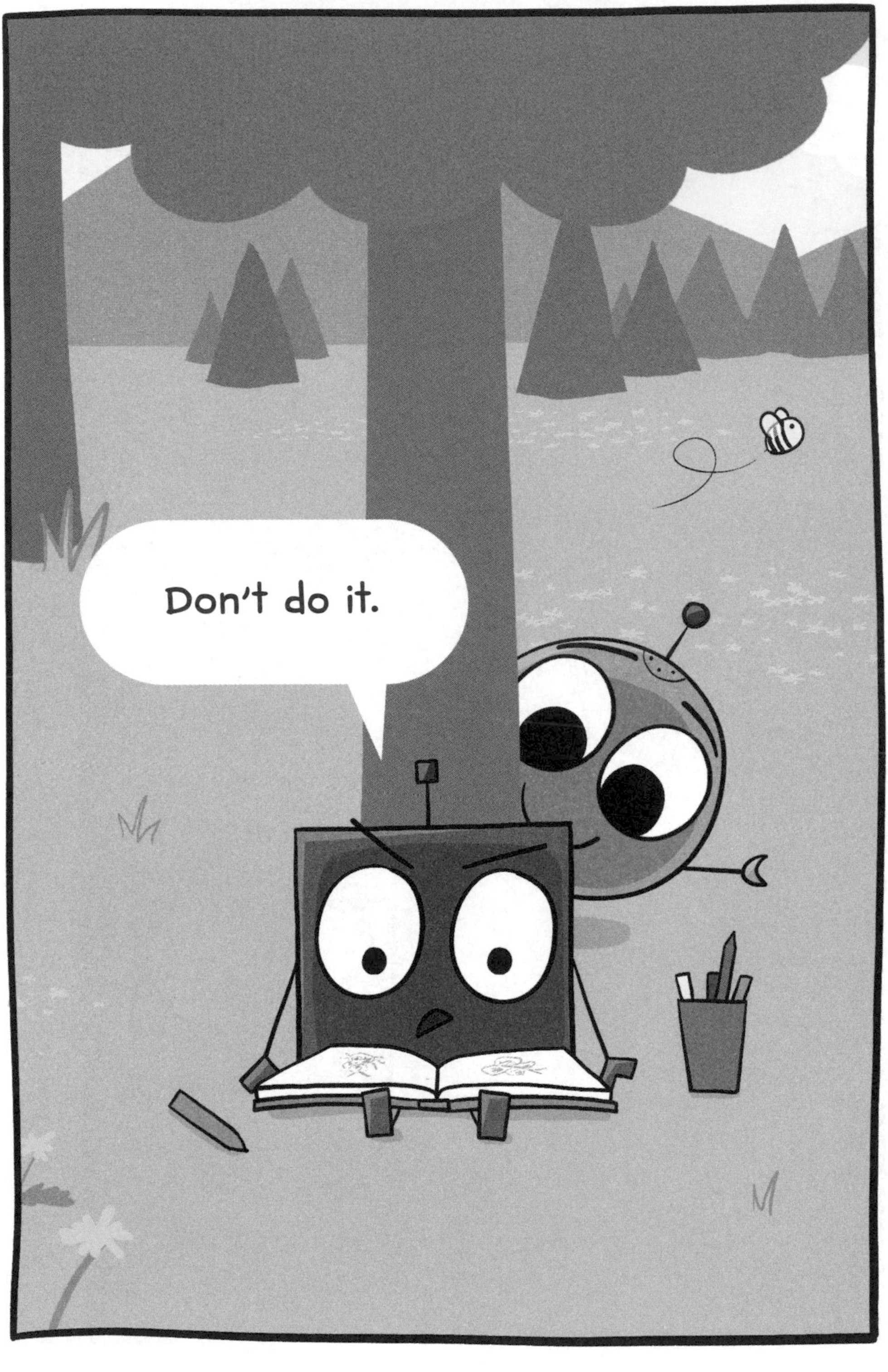
Don't do it.

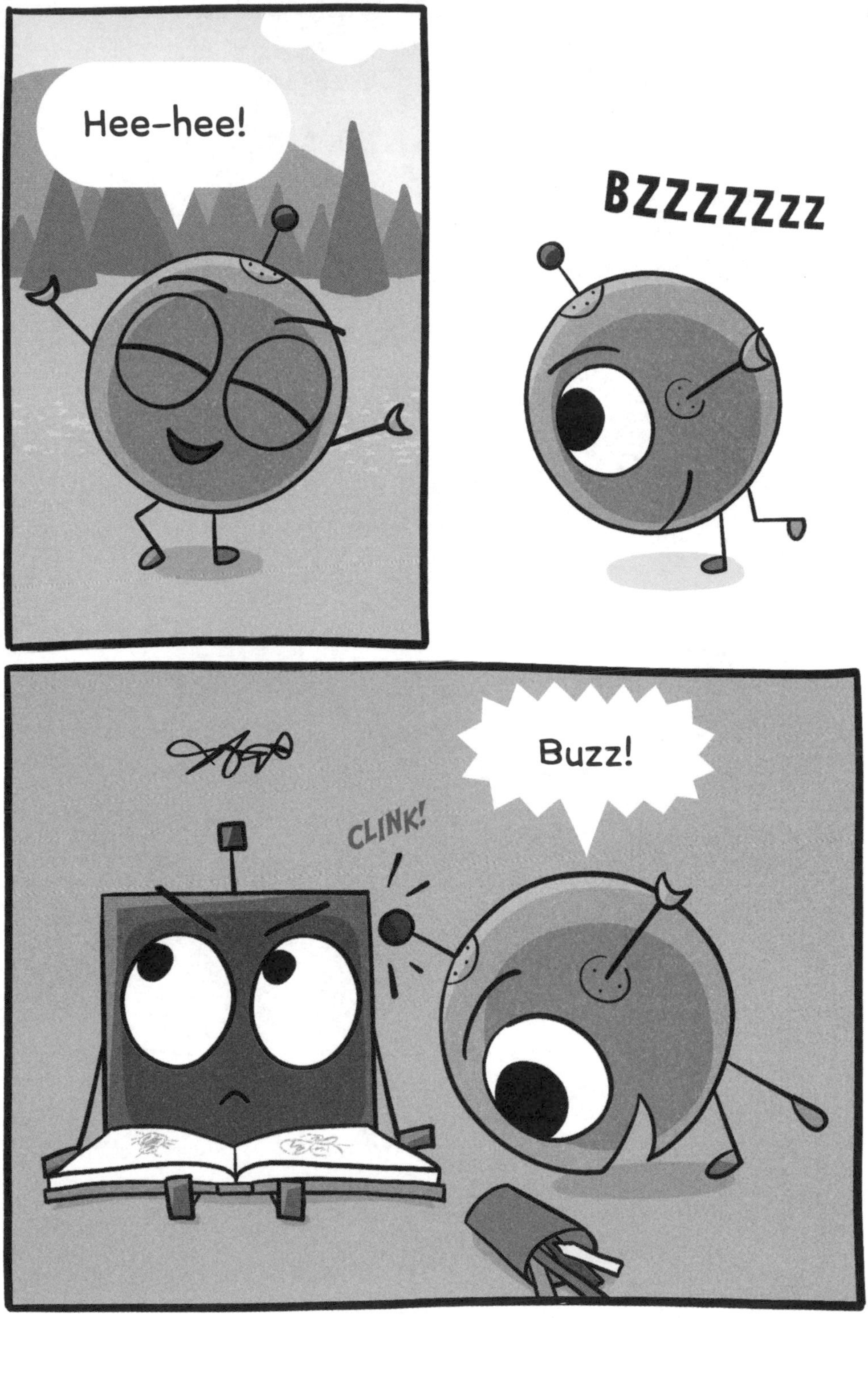

Hee-hee!
BZZZZZZZ
Buzz!
CLINK!

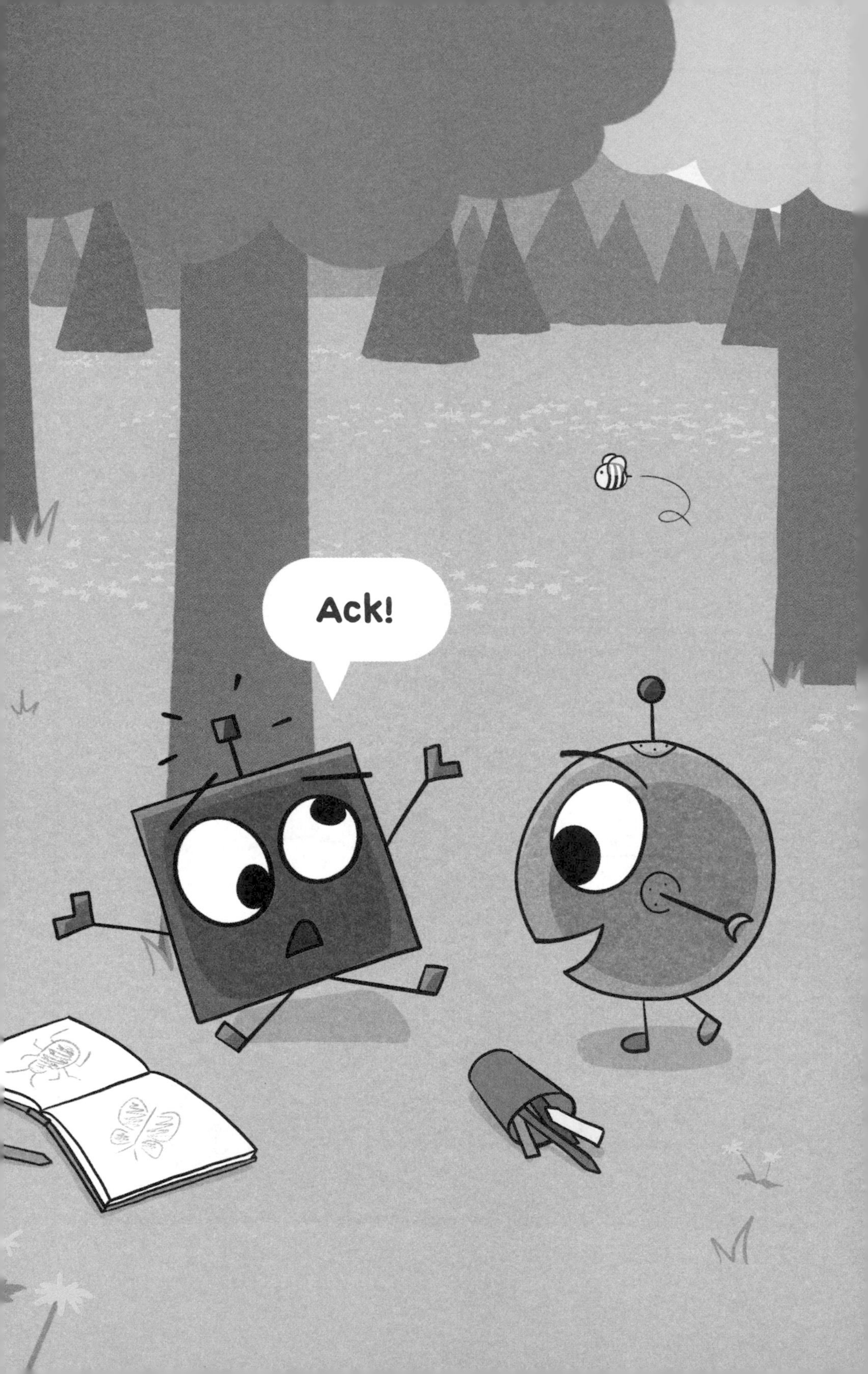
Ack!

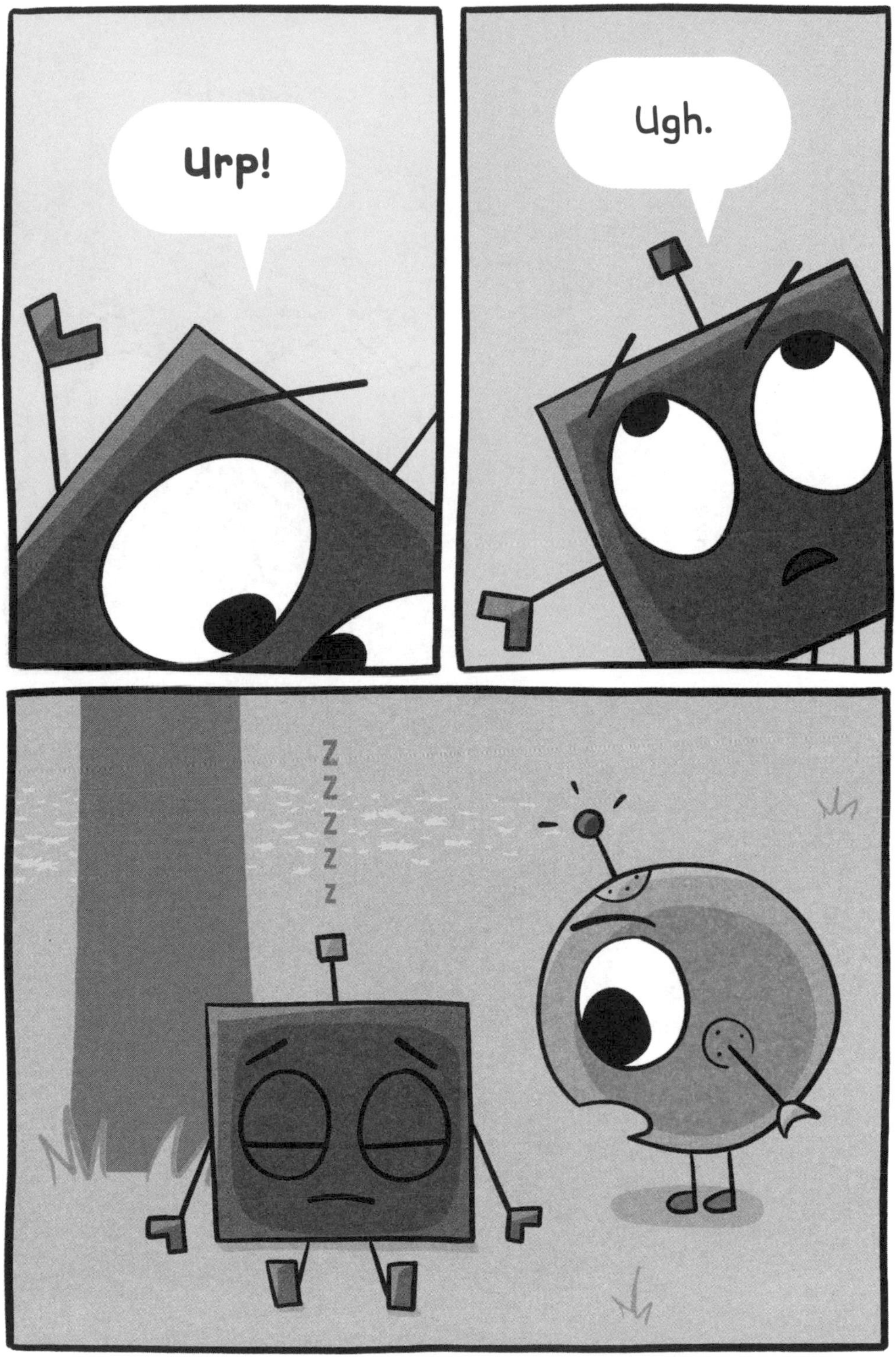
Urp!
Ugh.
Z
Z
Z
Z
Z

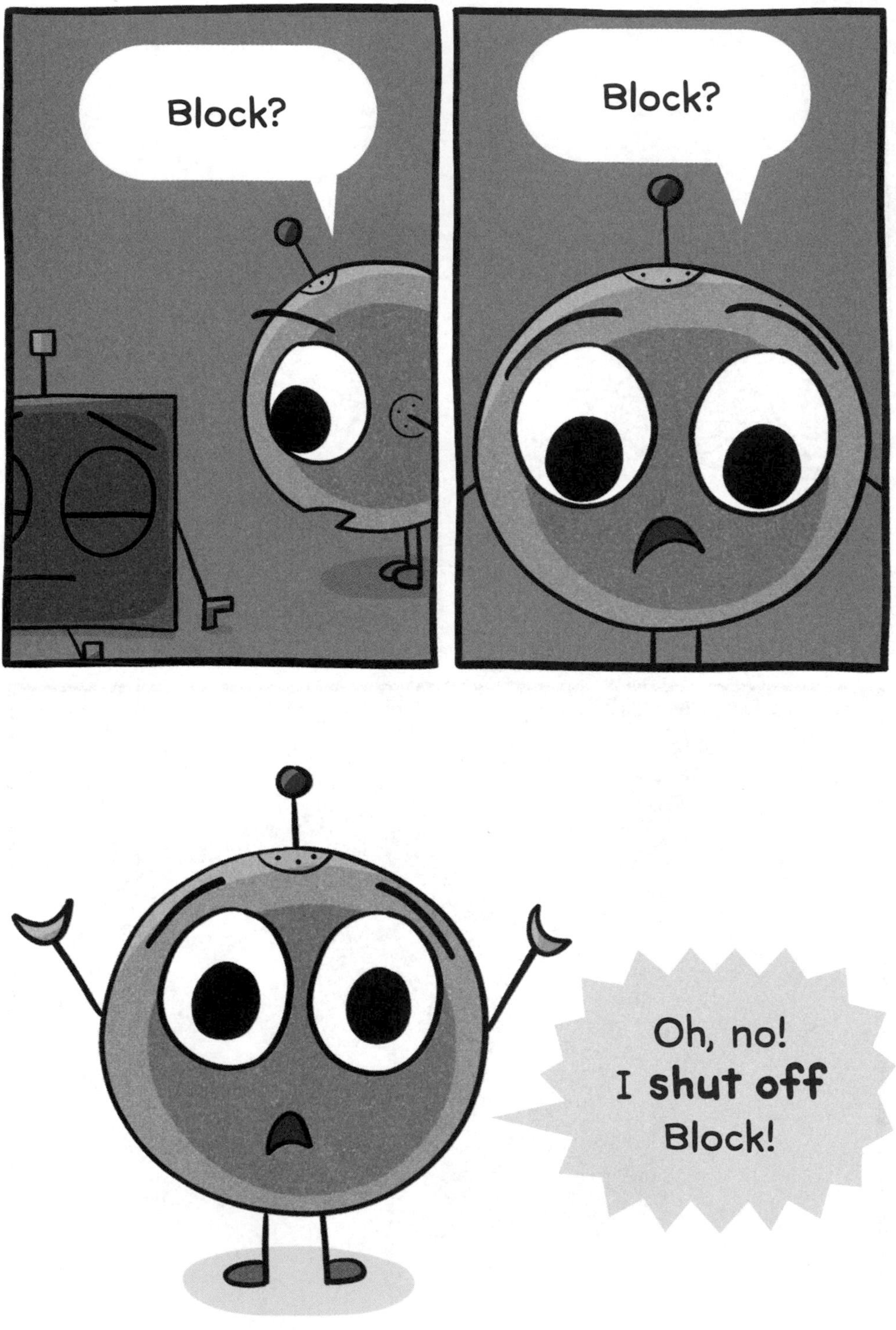
Block?
Block?
Oh, no! I **shut off** Block!

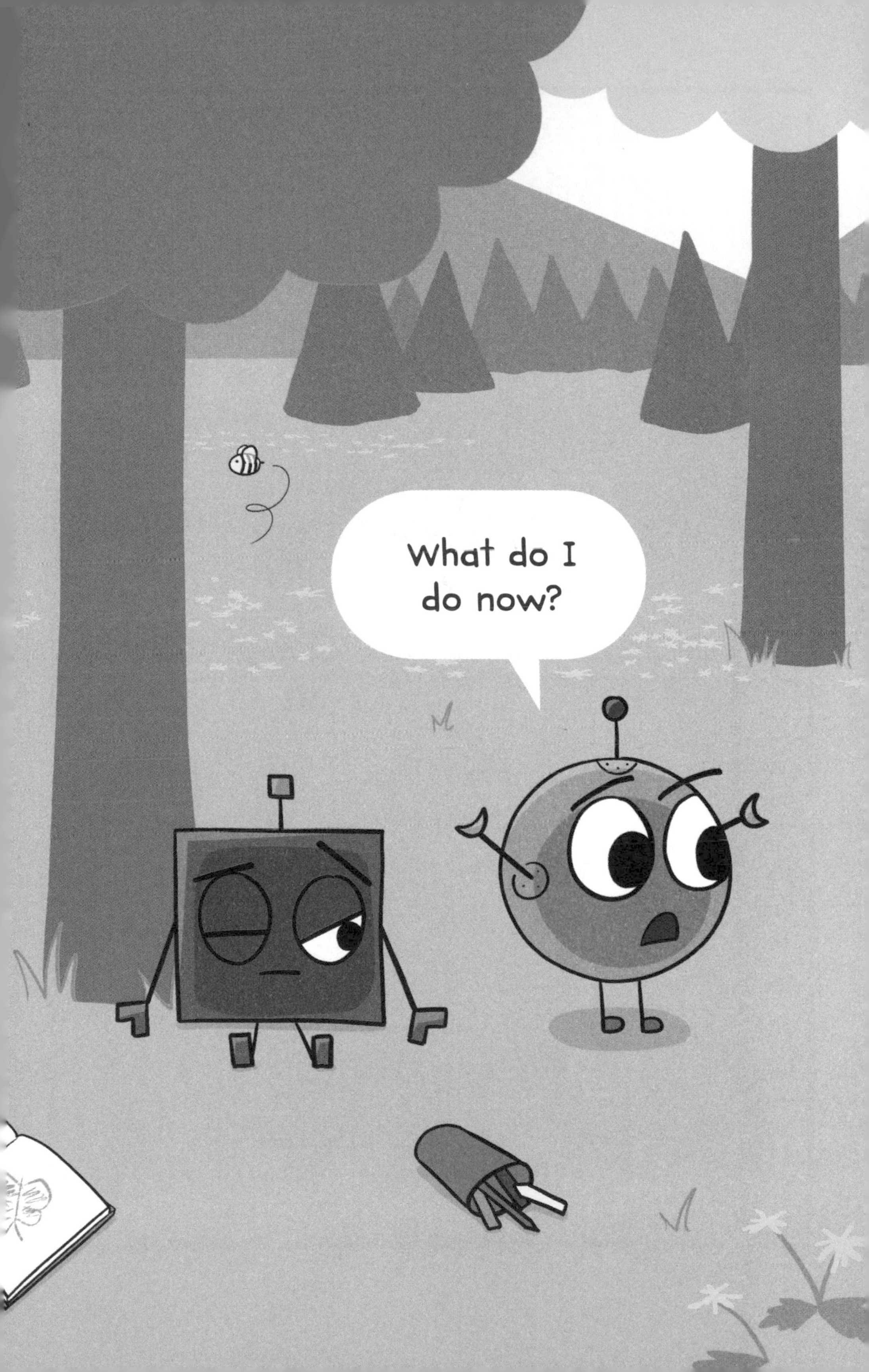
What do I do now?

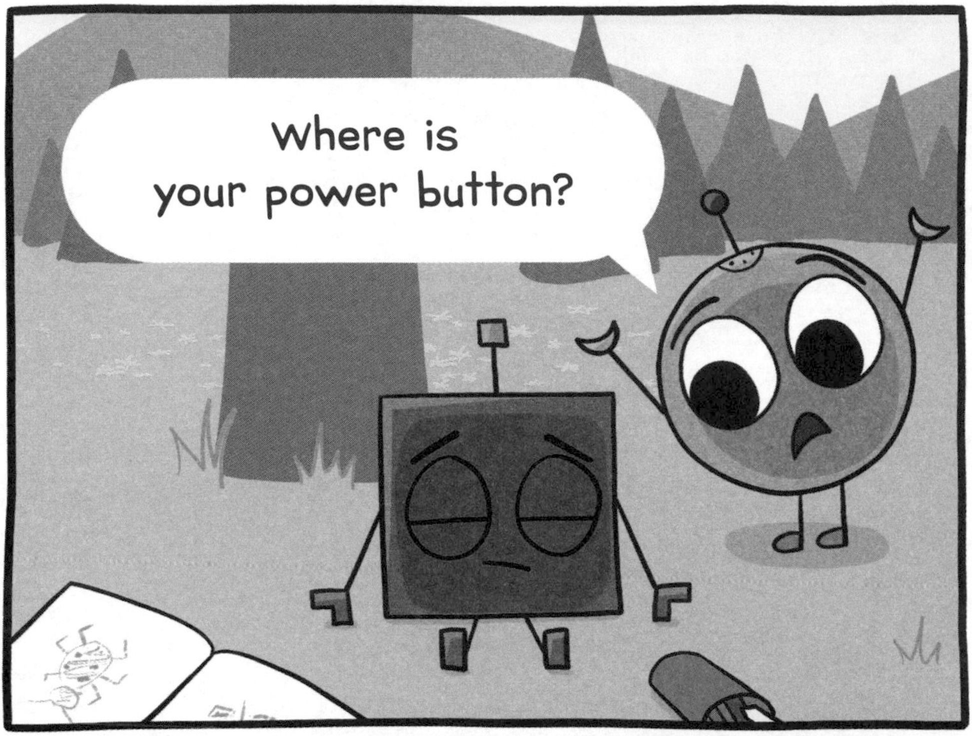
Where is your power button?

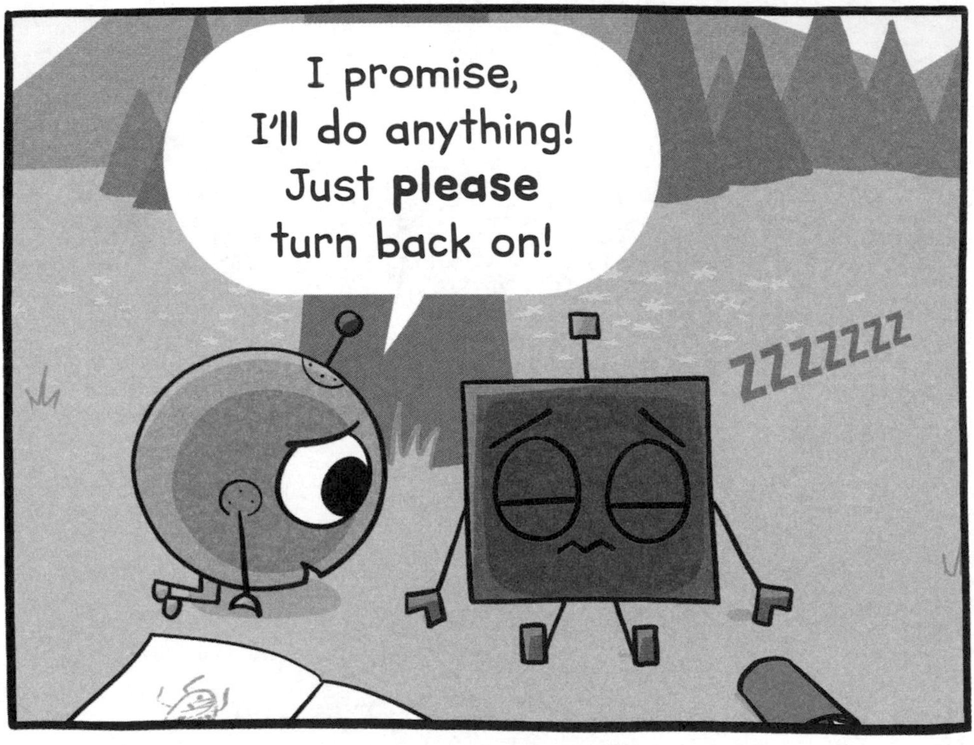
I promise, I'll do anything! Just **please** turn back on!
ZZZZZZZ

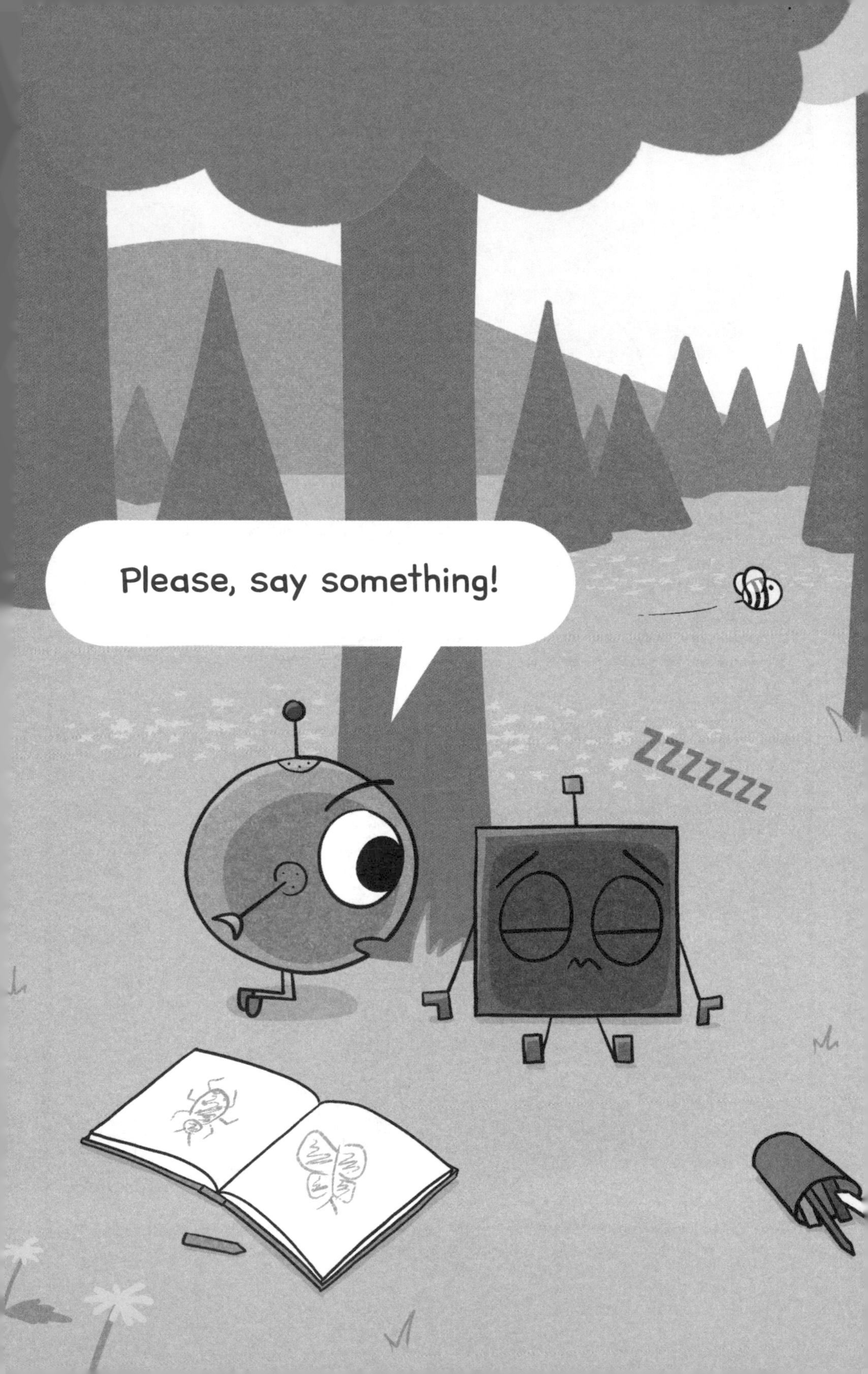
Please, say something!
ZZZZZZZ

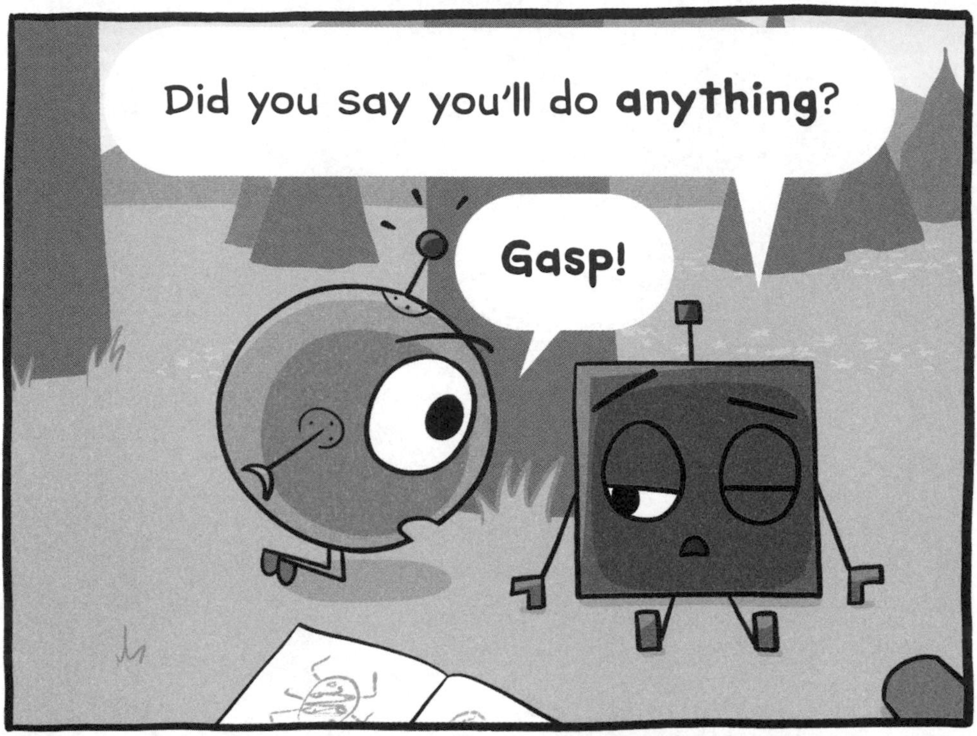
Did you say you'll do **anything**?
Gasp!

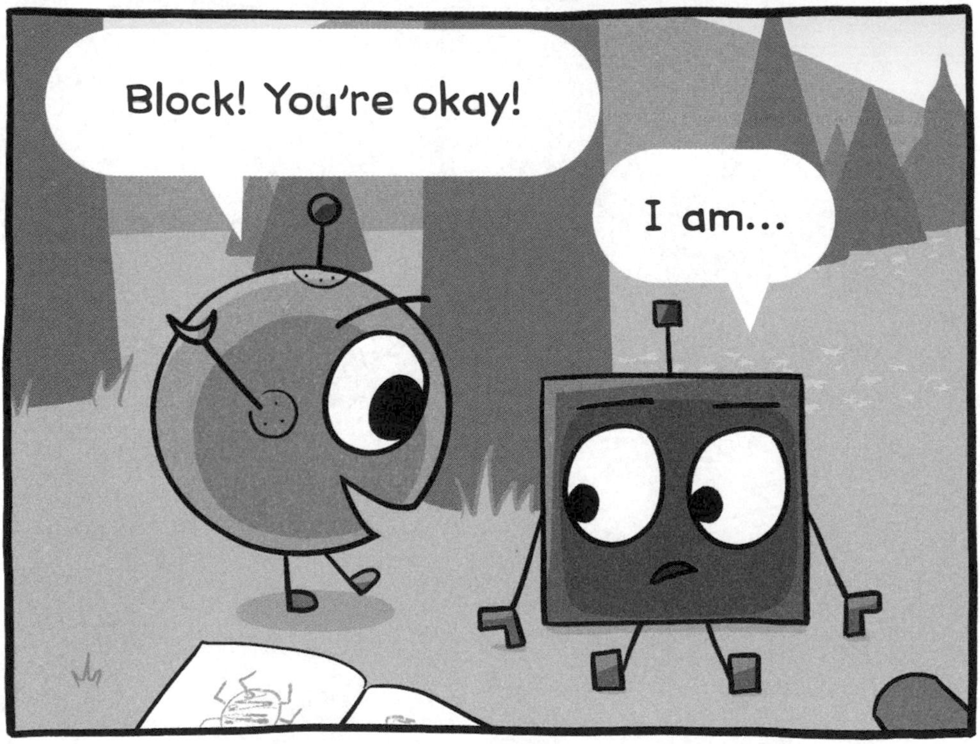
Block! You're okay!
I am...

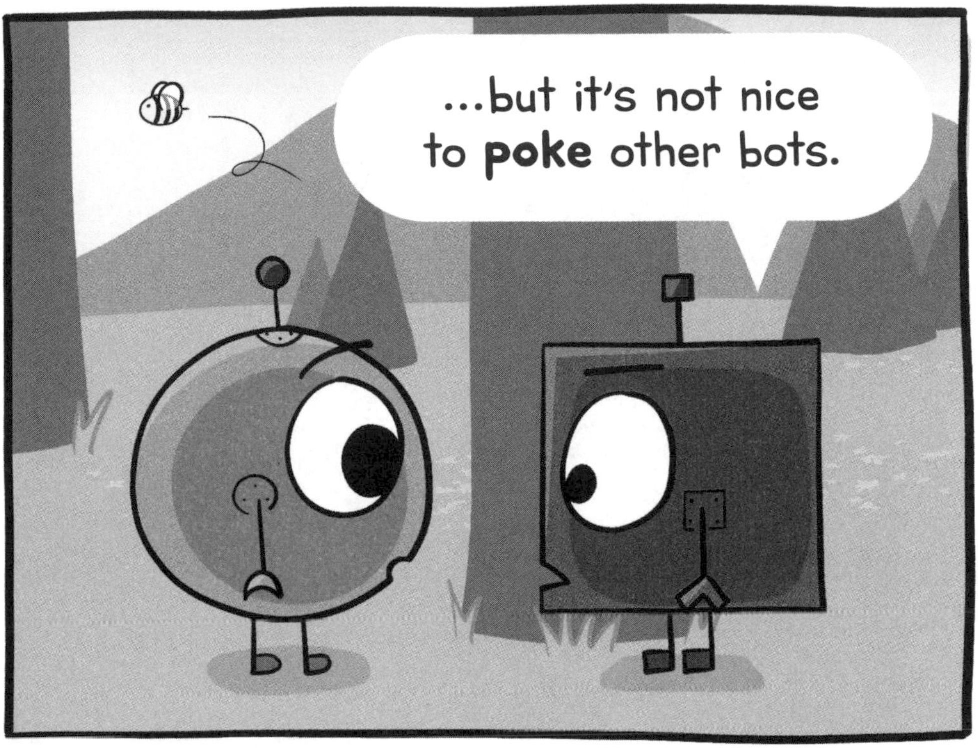
...but it's not nice to **poke** other bots.

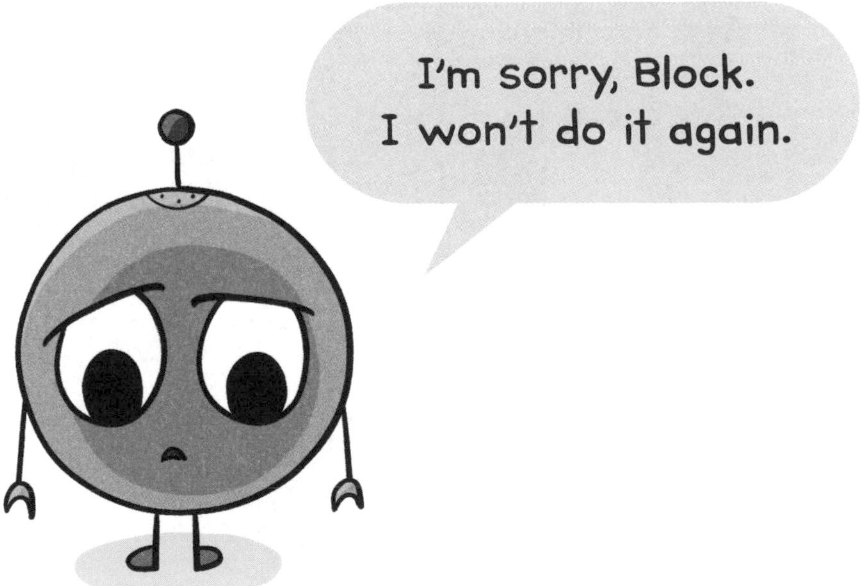
I'm sorry, Block. I won't do it again.

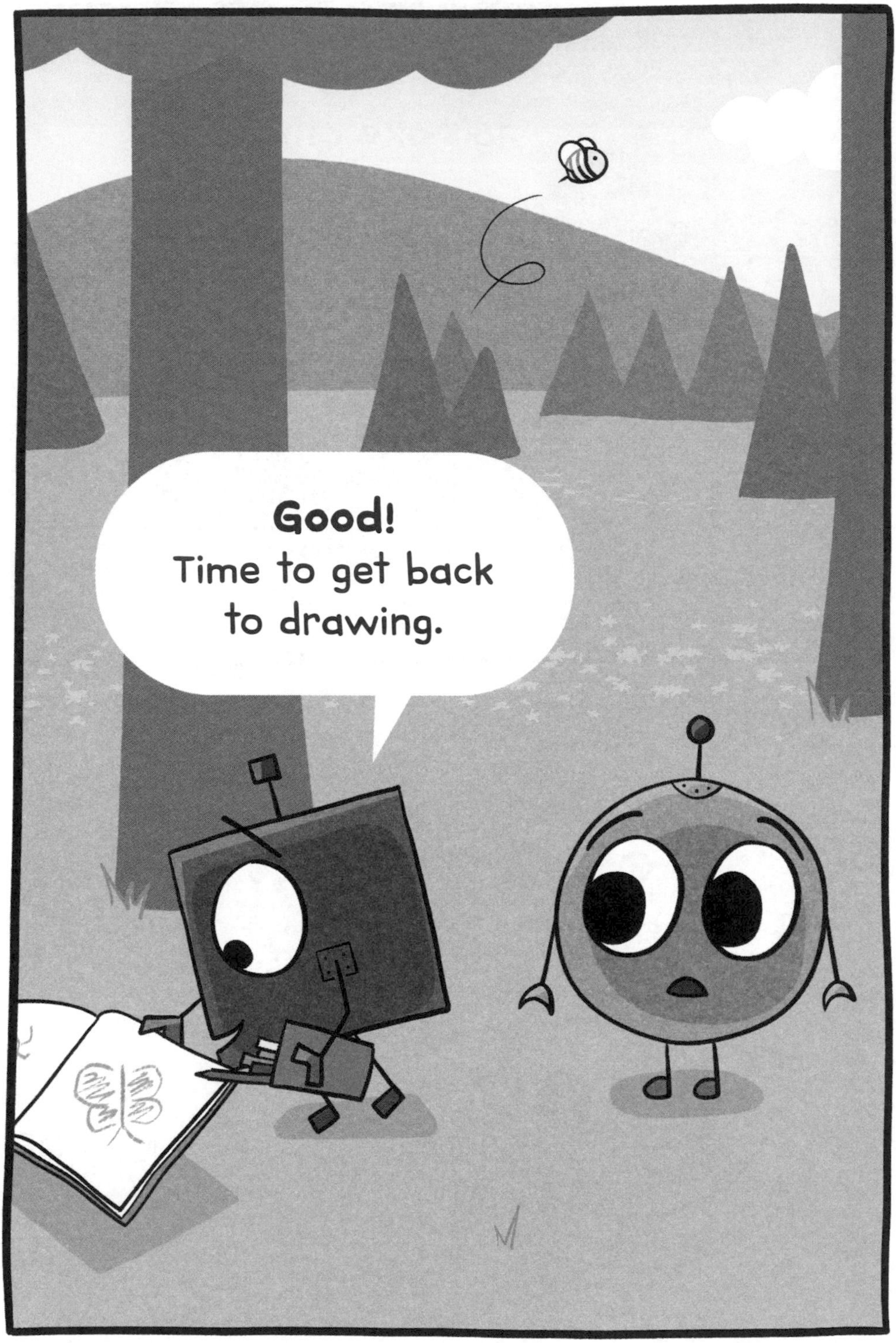
**Good!**
Time to get back
to drawing.

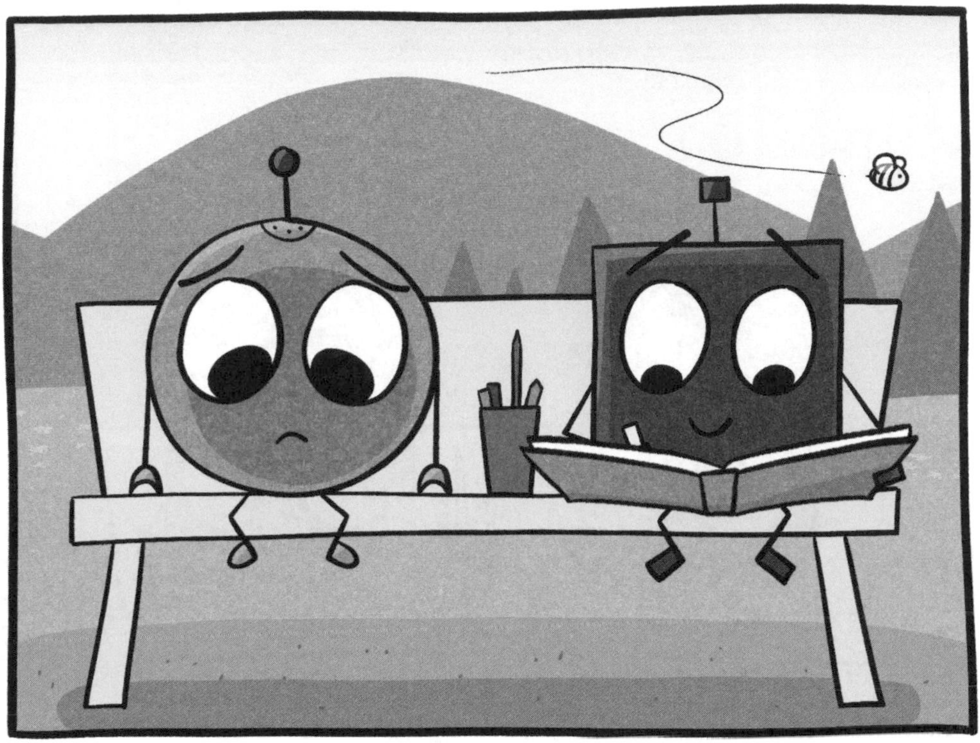

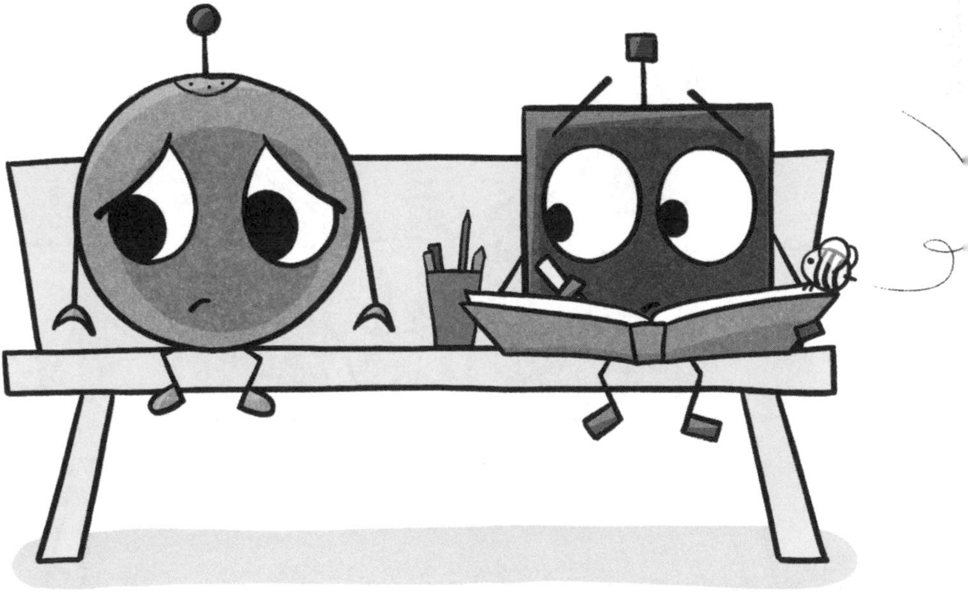

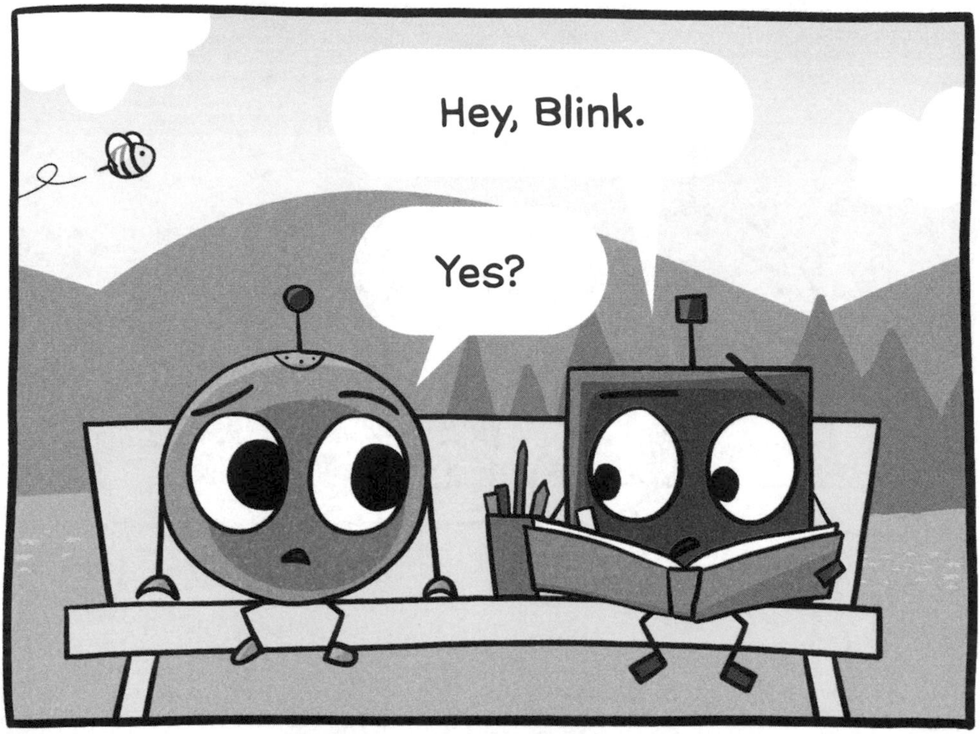
Hey, Blink.
Yes?

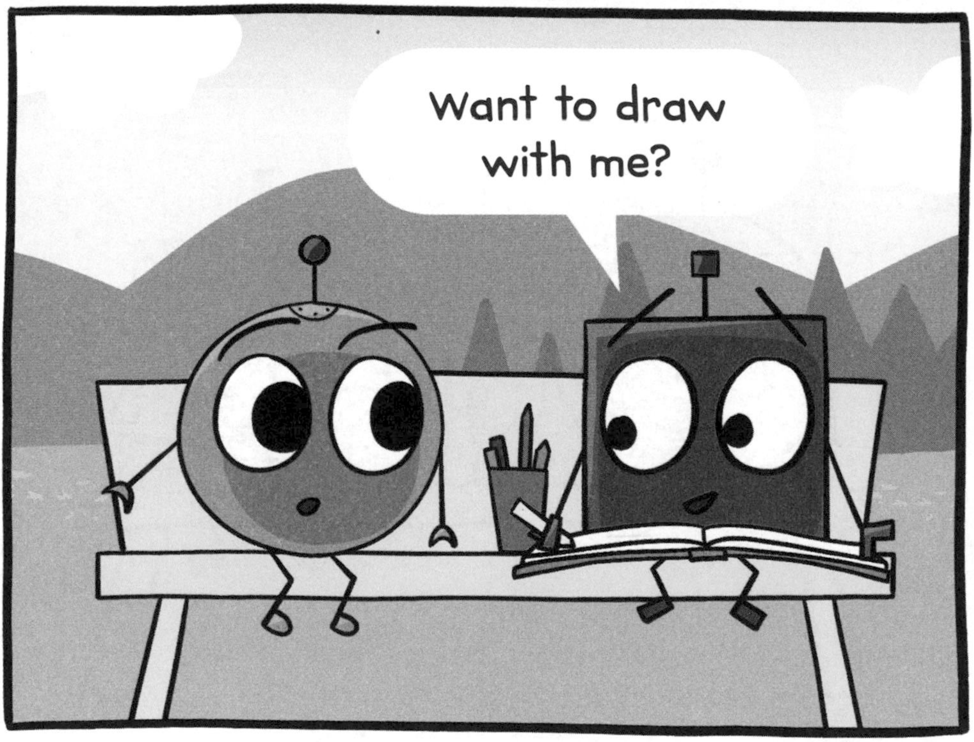
Want to draw with me?

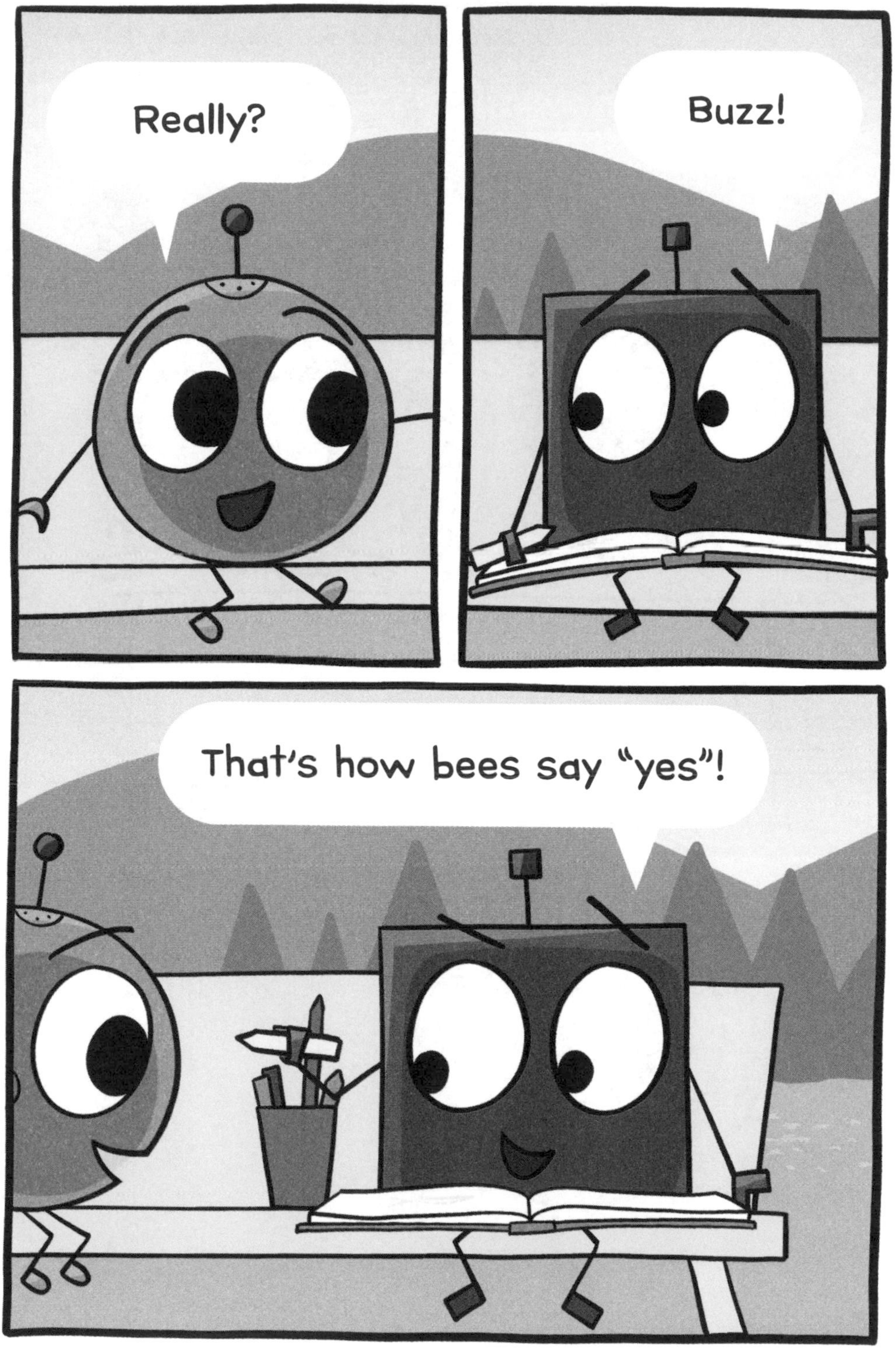
Really?
Buzz!
That's how bees say "yes"!

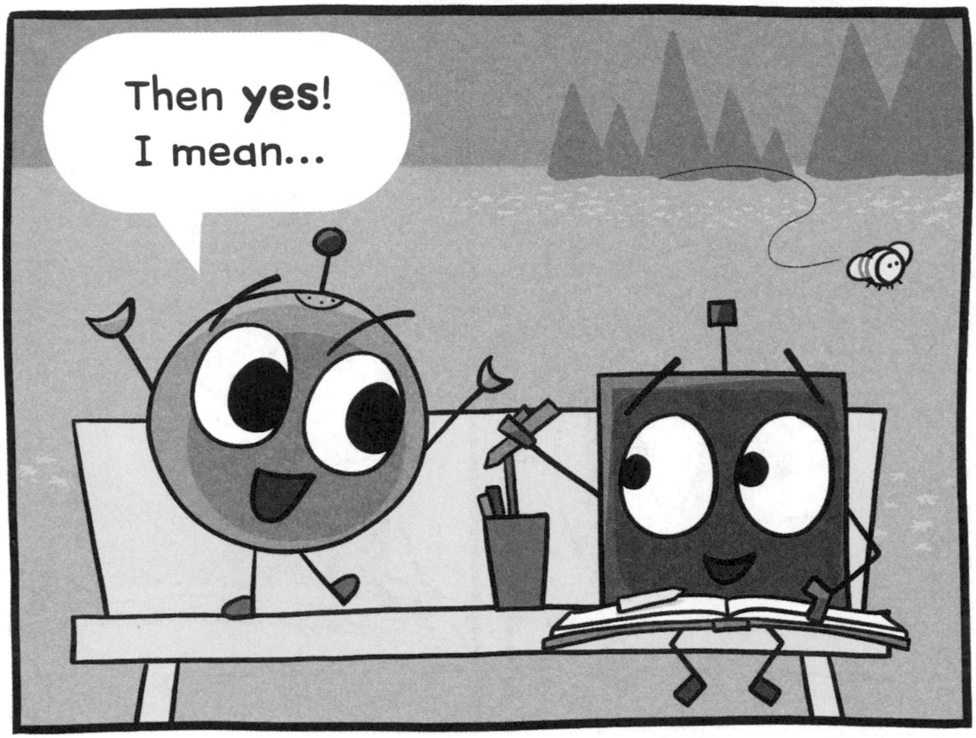
Then **yes**!
I mean...

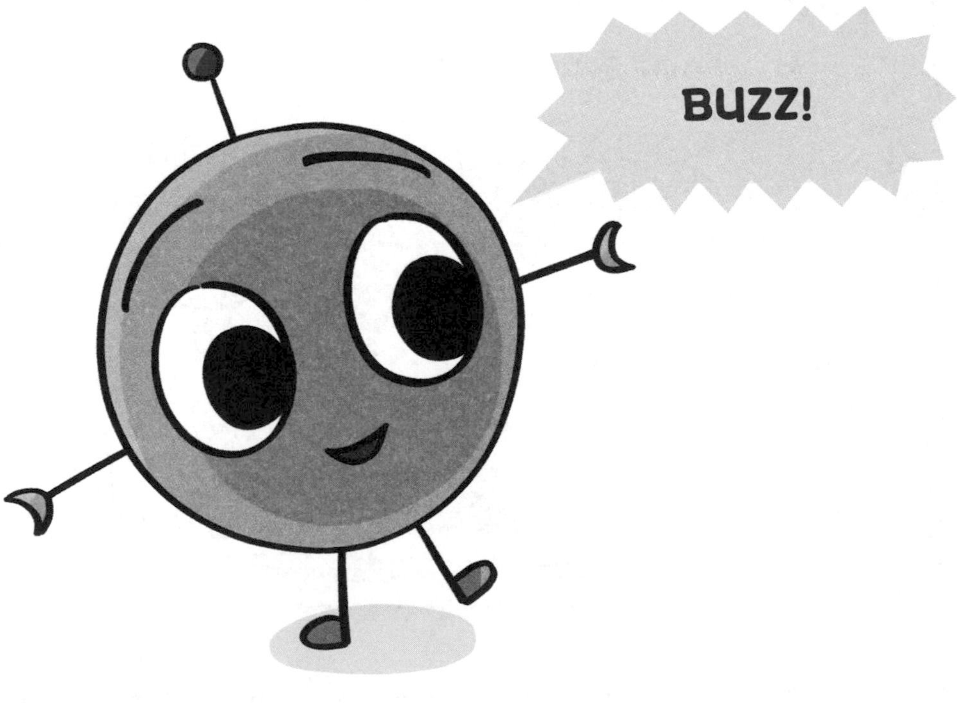
BUZZ!

# What is a BUTTON?

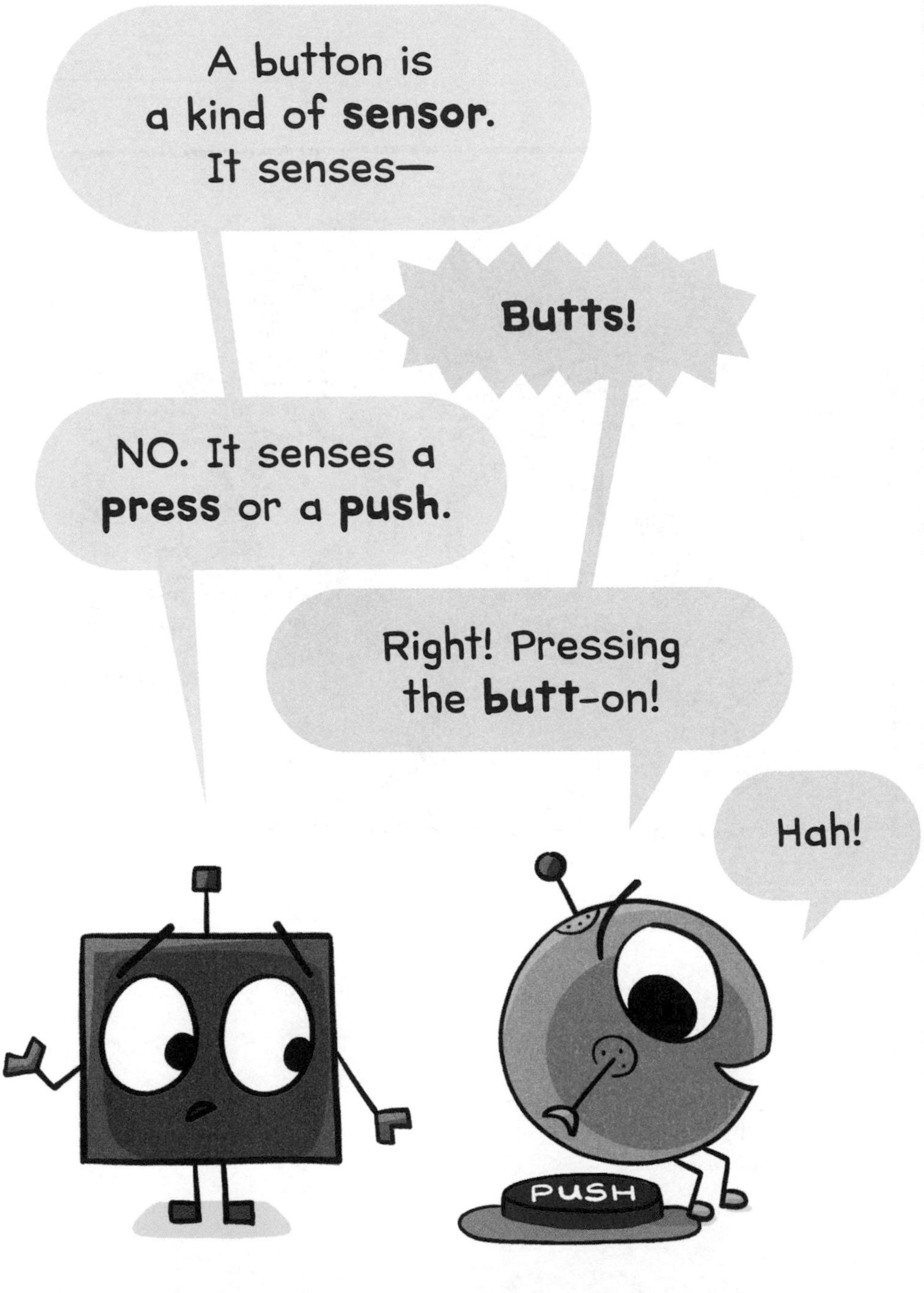
A button is a kind of **sensor**. It senses—
**Butts!**
NO. It senses a **press** or a **push**.
Right! Pressing the **butt**-on!
Hah!
PUSH